# Gypsy from Nowhere

# THEN THERE WAS GYPSY....

Wendy loved horses—yet horses were the reason for her fight against living on a ranch. Her father's new foreign assignment was only for a year, but to Wendy, the thought of spending even one year on a ranch, so close to the horses, was sheer torture.

Aunt Laura and Uncle Art were kind and sympathetic, of course, but they didn't really understand—about Buck and all.

Then there was Gypsy, a stunningly beautiful filly with one blue eye and one brown eye, who knew how to open doors—including the tightly locked door to Wendy's heart.

No one knew where Gypsy came from. She appeared at the Cross-R Ranch the same day Wendy arrived.

Gypsy and Wendy had other things in common, too. Each had something hidden in the past; each had been badly injured; each was afraid of people, afraid of being hurt again; each cried silently for understanding.

So it was natural that Wendy should be the only one who could rescue Gypsy. And it was just as natural that this courageous, intelligent horse—the gentle, shy, love-hungry *Gypsy From Nowhere*—should be the only one who could restore Wendy's happiness and self-confidence.

# Gypsy from Nowhere

By SHARON WAGNER

*Illustrated by Louis Cary*

*Cover by Jean Helmer*

 GOLDEN PRESS

Western Publishing Company, Inc.

Racine, Wisconsin

# Contents

1   Buck. . . . . . . . . . . . . . . . . . . . . . . . . . . . 11

2   Painful Memories . . . . . . . . . . . . . . . . 22

3   Ranch Life . . . . . . . . . . . . . . . . . . . . . 38

4   Mismatch . . . . . . . . . . . . . . . . . . . . . 51

5   Found and Lost. . . . . . . . . . . . . . . . . 67

6   Misfit . . . . . . . . . . . . . . . . . . . . . . . . . 77

7   The Only One . . . . . . . . . . . . . . . . . . . 90

8   Down and Out . . . . . . . . . . . . . . . . 102

9   Antisocial. . . . . . . . . . . . . . . . . . . . 120

10  Gypsy's Message. . . . . . . . . . . . . . . . 136

11  Ladybug, Ladybug . . . . . . . . . . . . . . 148

12  Horse Killer . . . . . . . . . . . . . . . . . . . 166

13  Blizzard!. . . . . . . . . . . . . . . . . . . . . . 181

14  One Blue Eye . . . . . . . . . . . . . . . . . 201

# 1 · Buck

WENDY McLYON stared from the plane window at the forest and mountains below—and hated them. Life was just too stupid to believe. Ever since she could remember, great things had seemed to happen at the wrong times, and this was surely the worst timing ever.

"I suppose we'll be arriving soon," observed the woman in the next seat.

"If the plane is on time," Wendy said. She would just as soon have it be late but felt sure that it would land exactly on schedule.

"I believe we're on schedule," the woman affirmed.

"It figures."

"I should think you'd be glad to be nearing the end of your journey," the woman said, with a slightly hurt note in her voice. "You've been on the plane a long time, haven't you?"

Wendy swallowed her bitterness and said, "I will be glad to get there—or at least to get off the plane. It's just that I don't want to be where I'm going, so. . . ." She let her words trail off, realizing that she shouldn't be talking this way to a stranger.

"You're young to be traveling alone, aren't you?" the woman asked.

"I'll be thirteen in September," Wendy said, trying not to think how long September was from April. "I've flown lots of times."

"Alone?"

Wendy nodded. "My father travels a lot in his business. Since my mother died, I've gone all around the western states to be with him when I can."

"Is he meeting you today?" the woman asked.

Wendy turned back to the window. "I didn't realize there were so many lakes here," she said.

The woman smiled. "There are quite a few in this part of Montana," she said. "We aren't far from Glacier National Park, you know. It's so beautiful. I really miss Montana when I'm away."

"It looks cold," Wendy said.

"This is only April," the woman chuckled, "hardly even spring yet."

"It was beautiful in Phoenix this morning," Wendy commented. "Warm and sunny—" She swallowed the lump that was growing in her throat. Phoenix wasn't the place to talk about now. If she started thinking about home so soon, she'd never be able to stand the months ahead.

"You'll get used to the climate," the woman said, turning her attention to the stewardess coming along the aisle to announce the end of their flight. Wendy turned once more to the window, preferring her thoughts to further conversation, though her thoughts were unhappy.

In the three years since her mother's death, Wendy had often talked and thought about coming to Montana to stay with her Uncle Art and Aunt Laura. That had been the plan at first, after her mother's death, when her father wasn't sure how well they could manage. But things had worked out, and Wendy had stayed in Phoenix. And, slowly, the idea of moving to the Montana ranch had faded.

Wendy squirmed uncomfortably, her leg and back aching more than ever. If she had come to Montana three years ago, when her dreams of

13

horses and ranches had been so real, everything would have worked out fine—she would never have had the accident. . . .

Her father's new foreign assignment was only for a year. But now Wendy couldn't bear the thought of spending even one year on a ranch, living so close to the horses.

"Where are you going?" the woman asked, breaking into her thoughts once more.

"The Cross-R Ranch," Wendy answered. "It's near Littleville."

"The Roush place? Surely you're not a guest so early in the season."

"Do you know the Roushes?" Now it was Wendy's turn to be curious. "They're my aunt and uncle. I'm going to live with them for a while."

"In this part of the country, everybody knows everybody else. I expect the whole lake basin knows you're coming. You must be Lisa's little girl."

Wendy nodded, though it seemed strange to hear her mother's name from a stranger. "Did you know my mother?" she asked.

"I went to school with her and your Aunt Laura. I lost touch with Lisa after she married, but I did hear about you from your aunt. I was sorry to hear about your mother's death."

"She was sick for quite a while," Wendy said softly.

"So you're going to be staying at the Cross-R. . . . I'm sure you'll love it. A lot of girls your age want to work there in the summer; the Roushes are so nice."

Wendy didn't quite know what to say to that. Just then the pilot's voice came over the speakers; they were about to land.

The woman busied herself with her purse and tote bag, leaving Wendy free to look down at the small town below. It looked lonely in the midst of all the trees—almost as lonely as Wendy felt.

The plane settled onto the landing strip with a thud, then taxied between towering pines to the long, low terminal building. Wendy stood up when the motors stopped but didn't push her way out into the aisle with the other passengers. Even now, six weeks after her accident, her leg and back were too tender for hurrying.

"You'll need this," the stewardess said, pulling Wendy's coat down from the overhead rack. "It's a lot colder here than it was in Phoenix."

15

"Thank you," Wendy said, shrugging her way into the coat and lifting her pale brown hair outside the collar. The plane was now almost empty, with only the two stewardesses moving efficiently about. It was time to go, Wendy realized. Her arrival couldn't be postponed any longer.

Limping only slightly, Wendy made her way along the aisle and down the metal stairway. The wind, iced by nearby snow-covered peaks, tugged at her hair and brought tears to her eyes as she surveyed the crowd on the other side of the fence. Would she recognize them? she asked herself for the hundredth time. It had been six years since she had seen her aunt and uncle. She'd been just a child when they had visited in Phoenix.

"Gwendolyn! Over here, dear."

Wendy winced at the sound of her full name but turned obediently. Her smile was forced as she recognized her aunt and uncle. It wasn't their fault that things had changed, she reminded herself. They thought she still wanted to come to Montana, just as Daddy thought. No one knew how she really felt, except Dr. Mike, and he hadn't been the slightest bit sympathetic.

16

"Fear is the only thing you have to conquer now, Wendy," he'd said on her last visit. "Your back and leg are doing fine. The pain you have is in your mind. It won't be easy, but I think you'll get over your fear of horses. You will try, won't you?"

She'd agreed then, Wendy thought grimly, but that had been before she knew the whole awful truth about what had happened.

She pushed the bleak memories away and forced herself to concentrate on the greetings and questions from her aunt and uncle. It wasn't till she was in the station wagon with them that she had time to feel nervous again.

"I can't tell you how much we've been looking forward to this, Gwendolyn," her aunt said.

"Please—call me Wendy. I've always thought Gwendolyn was a name for a fat cat on a satin pillow."

Uncle Art laughed easily. "Wendy it is," he said. "You are no fat cat. But we could keep you on a satin pillow for a while and fatten you up."

"I haven't had much appetite since the accident," Wendy admitted.

"You've had a bad time," Aunt Laura agreed, "but living on the ranch will help, I'm sure. Your

17

father said that the doctor recommended lots of exercise and fresh air."

"A year of riding and working with the guests will have you so healthy your father won't recognize you," Uncle Art said heartily.

Wendy shuddered. "No riding," she said in a small voice. "I mean, after what happened—"

"Riding accidents can happen to anyone," Aunt Laura said. "Yours *was* serious, but you're better now."

"I thought you were the girl who loved horses more than anything," Uncle Art said.

"I did, but—" Wendy had a sinking feeling that they didn't really understand how she felt.

"Your father told us that you and a horse you were riding were hit by a car," Aunt Laura said.

Wendy could see the sympathy in her eyes. She nodded but couldn't speak as the whole horrible scene filled her mind like a black cloud. Once more she felt the cold, early-morning air and smelled the damp, earthy scent of the Arizona citrus grove.

She hadn't been away from the stable long, and Buck was still bouncing with energy. The man at the stable had cautioned Wendy to be careful with Buck, not to ride him outside the

18

stable area. But she'd been so sure of herself, so full of dreams of having Buck for her own, that she hadn't paid any attention. . . .

"Did it change your feelings about horses?" Uncle Art asked. "Do you blame the one you were riding?"

"Oh, no," Wendy said, horrified that he might think such a thing. "It wasn't Buck's fault. He was frightened by a tractor beside the road, and I just wasn't a good enough rider to hold him back. He bolted into the side of a pickup truck." Wendy shivered, though it was warm inside the station wagon.

She could still feel the lunge and the horrible jolt of impact. She could hear the horse's cry and a scream of her own as the animal fell, crushing her leg beneath him and twisting her back into an arc of white-hot pain. . . .

Wendy reached down and began rubbing the tensed muscles around her right knee. Though her pantsuit hid the marks, she could feel how thin this leg had become, compared to the other. She remembered the three weeks she'd lain in the hospital, not sure that her leg was going to heal properly, wondering how her back would be and if she could ever walk normally again.

19

"I know how hard it is to get back on a horse once you've been hurt," Uncle Art said, forcing her to stop thinking of the past, "but you have to, Wendy. It's easier if you do it right away, of course, but with your broken leg and your back injury— Well, you'll be able to do it now."

"You'll have plenty of gentle horses to try," Aunt Laura agreed. "In fact, we have more gentle horses than anything else, I think."

Wendy wanted to scream at them, to tell them that it didn't matter if the horse was gentle or not. "I don't know," she said softly after a moment. "I don't *want* to be afraid, but I can't seem to help it. Besides, my back is still awfully weak, and I don't think riding would be good for it."

Wendy didn't miss the long look that passed between her aunt and uncle, but she was grateful when neither of them said anything more. At least it was over for the moment. She'd told them as much as they needed to know. After all her years of dreaming and wanting a horse of her own, she'd finally admitted to herself that it could never be.

"I talked to Peg Carter today," her aunt said, changing the subject.

20

"Who?" Wendy asked.

"The junior high teacher who is going to tutor you. She's quite sure you can make up all the work you missed because of your accident."

"I won't have to go to school for the rest of the year, will I?" Wendy asked, sure that she could never face a classroom full of strangers. She hadn't even been able to face the questions in her old friends' eyes.

"That will depend on your progress, I imagine," her aunt said. "If you can make up enough work, you may be able to take your final tests with the class."

"I'd rather take them alone," Wendy said.

"You may change your mind after a while. Your father told us that you had a little problem going back to school right after you got out of the hospital. But six weeks can make a big difference. Once you make friends. . . ."

Her aunt's tone told Wendy that her father hadn't really explained what had happened. She tried to find the words herself, but none came.

"Welcome to the Cross-R," her uncle said as he turned off the highway. They bounced over a cattle guard and onto a narrow gravel road. "You can't see the house yet, but this is our land."

21

## 2 · *Painful Memories*

UNCLE ART drove very slowly. Wendy wondered why, until they rounded one of the many blind corners and found the road blocked by a Hereford cow and her little red and white calf. Uncle Art honked and then laughed as the calf disappeared into the trees like a flash while his mother lumbered after him. "We'll get the stock out of this part of the ranch before the guests start arriving," he said. "But I like to keep the cattle in close while they're calving."

"Do you have a lot of cattle?" Wendy asked nervously. Seeing the animal in front of the car that way had set her heart pounding.

"Not by ranching standards," Uncle Art said, "but, between the horses, cattle, and summer guests, it's enough for a reasonable living."

"Or it would be—if he'd stop *buying* horses

and start *selling* them," Aunt Laura said, with a teasing note in her voice. "Every time I turn around, our profits disappear on four legs."

"When you hear what I get for the horses I sell this year," he said, "you'll see that it pays to buy the best. Thing is, Wendy, I've been building a herd of Appaloosas, and it takes time to develop exactly what I want."

"Don't let him get started on his Appaloosas," Aunt Laura warned, "or you'll be hearing the pedigree of every one of his mares—and the detailed future of each foal."

Wendy found herself smiling, in spite of her doubts. "I don't mind," she said. "I still like horses; it's just that I don't want to ride them. I don't mind being around them or talking about them."

"Well, it may be pure selfishness on my part," Aunt Laura said, "but I'm not one bit sorry you won't be spending all day every day in the saddle. I've always wanted a daughter to do things with, and I've looked forward to having you here."

In spite of her resolve not to care too much for her aunt and uncle, Wendy felt a stirring. "What kinds of things, Aunt Laura?" she asked.

"Well, if you're interested, I thought we could sew and knit and maybe redecorate the oldest of the cabins. It's beginning to look a little shabby, now that the other two are done."

"I'm afraid I don't know much about knitting or sewing, but if you don't mind a slow pupil, I'd like to learn," Wendy said. "Mom never had much time to teach me things like that. By the time I was old enough to be interested, she was sick, and—"

"Well, there it is," Uncle Art said, stopping the station wagon on a little rise so that Wendy could see the view. "The building in front is the house and garage; the three smaller ones behind it are the guest cabins. Each one has two little bedrooms and a small living room but no cooking facilities. The guests eat with us. The barn you can see, and the small building behind it is the bunkhouse. I have two hands working for me—Cliff and George. They're away for the weekend, but you'll meet them on Monday."

"It's bigger than I expected," Wendy said, her eyes drawn at once to the complexity of corrals that stretched out around the barn. There were cattle in the largest corral, and two others contained horses.

"The cabin closest to the barn is where we lived first," Aunt Laura said. "We built the big house six years ago and added the other two cabins the following year." She paused, turning to Wendy with a smile. "I hope you like your room," she said. "I didn't know what your tastes would be, but I wanted to have a place ready for you."

"I'm sure it will be fine," Wendy said, still looking toward the barn as her uncle drove down the hill and across the meadow toward the house. The drive circled between the house and the barn, then turned back to pass grandly between two tall sentinel pines that guarded the house. Uncle Art drove right up to the house, then jumped out to unlock the back door.

"This really isn't an elegant way to enter," Aunt Laura said, "but it's quicker this way. Our winter seems a long way from being over."

Wendy slid out of the car, favoring her bad leg a little, then forgetting it entirely as a large calico cat stepped in front of her. Round, golden eyes regarded Wendy solemnly for several seconds, and then the cat meowed and began winding her soft body around Wendy's legs.

"That's Abigail," Aunt Laura said. "She really

25

should stay in the barn with the other animals, but she's due to have kittens any day now, and she's gotten rather independent."

"She's pretty," Wendy said, kneeling down to stroke the cat. "Do you have lots of cats? Are there any dogs? I've lived mostly in apartments, so I couldn't have any pets."

"We had a shepherd," Uncle Art said as he unloaded her two suitcases and started into the house with them. "But he died last fall, and we haven't found another dog yet. Maybe that can be your department. There are always people with puppies around here. When you find one you like, we'll get it."

Wendy felt a warm glow of excitement at the suggestion, but it faded as she remembered Buffy and Mittens. She'd had them a long time ago, when she was little, but the hurt still lingered. Buffy, the puppy, had been first, when they were living in Oregon. She'd had him for nearly a year before they'd moved and she'd had to give him away.

Mittens, the kitten, had lived with them for only six months before Wendy had to give her up, but it hadn't hurt any less. She'd never asked for another pet after that.

Wendy swallowed hard, reminding herself that she'd only be here for a year, and at the end of that time. . . . She tried to step around Abigail, but the cat was persistent, and finally Wendy had to pick her up.

With Abigail purring happily in her arms, Wendy followed her aunt and uncle into the bright, delicious-smelling kitchen. Finished in light wood, with sunny yellow counters and green and yellow checked curtains, it was a happy room, and Wendy couldn't help responding to it.

In spite of her feeling about horses, her depression was lifting a little. Her aunt and uncle had been more understanding of her fears than she'd expected, so maybe—just maybe—things would work out for the year she must stay.

"Your room is down here," Aunt Laura said. "It's next to the kitchen. I'm afraid it might be a bit noisy, but the other bedroom is so small, I was sure you'd like this one better." She led Wendy through the swinging doors into a large rustic dining room that contained four medium-sized plank tables with matching benches. Then she passed into a hallway, stopping at the first door. She opened it, switched on the lights, and stepped back to allow Wendy to go in alone.

For a moment Wendy couldn't believe her eyes. From what she had seen of the kitchen and dining room, she'd expected western-style furnishings in her room—perhaps even bunk beds. But she couldn't have been more wrong.

A blue tweed rug covered the floor and set off the white and gold bedroom furniture perfectly. A bed, twin nightstands, a big bureau, and a small, graceful dressing table were tastefully arranged. In one corner were a small desk and a straight chair, forming a study nook. The bedspread and drapes were printed with gay green, white, and blue designs, and the dressing table stool and the chair had cushions covered with the same material.

"Do you like it?" Aunt Laura asked. "If you don't, we can get different material for the bedspread and drapes."

"Like it?" Suddenly Wendy burst into tears as all of her fears and uncertainties melted in the warmth of love that seemed to flow through the room. She was conscious of her aunt's arm on her shoulder, gently guiding her to the bed. Behind her, she heard her uncle's questions and Aunt Laura's soft assurances.

28

"I think you need a little time to relax," her aunt said gently. "I have a casserole in the oven, so I'll finish fixing dinner. You can come out when you're ready, okay?"

Wendy nodded gratefully.

After a few minutes, her tears stopped, and she looked around. There were two doors opposite her bed—one opened into a large closet, the other into a small bathroom. Pausing only long enough to wash the tearstains from under her dark blue eyes, Wendy went back to explore the room. After years of living in apartments or traveling with her father, it seemed strange to have a room specially prepared just for her.

A soft sound brought her attention away from the furnishings, and she looked toward the big window. It faced in the direction they'd come from, but the highway wasn't visible because of the forest. Abigail, apparently shut in the room with Wendy when Aunt Laura left, was standing on the windowsill, meowing softly.

"Do you want out, Abigail?" Wendy asked, noting that the window had no screen.

Abigail purred her answer, obviously appreciative of Wendy's solicitude.

Wendy opened the window and leaned out to

29

sniff the cold, damp air as she watched the calico cat picking her way around the side of the house. Montana *was* beautiful, Wendy thought, staring across the high meadow grass toward the trees—not in the same way that the desert was beautiful, but impressive in its own special way.

A sudden movement caught her eye. Something was coming out of the trees across the meadow. *Probably one of the cows*, Wendy thought, watching the shadows carefully. Then her breath caught in her throat. A horse—a young one, probably no more than a yearling but already beautifully proportioned—picked its way daintily through the tall grass, pausing once or twice to crop a mouthful of grass. It paused and looked her way, head high, ears sharply pricked forward.

A sound from the house broke the almost magical stillness, and the horse spun and leaped away like a frightened deer, disappearing into the trees. Wendy waited, hoping to catch another glimpse, perhaps farther down the edge of the meadow, but after several minutes, she knew she wasn't going to. Shivering a bit from the cold wind, she closed the window and retreated to the bed.

What was she doing, hanging out the window to stare at a horse? she asked herself. Why couldn't she just forget horses? Why couldn't she ignore them, the way her mother and father had done? After the accident, it was obvious that Wendy was never meant to ride or have her own horse.

Fighting her longing to go back to the window and watch for the horse, Wendy opened her suitcases and started to unpack. The activity was no escape from her memories, though. Instead, they crowded around her, as if summoned by the sorrel she'd just seen. Visions of Buck flooded her mind.

Buck had been her favorite horse at the riding stable in Arizona. The stable was owned by her best friend's father, and he had given Wendy riding lessons so that she and Gretchen could ride together.

Buck was too high-spirited for a beginner, so Wendy had ridden several of the other horses at first. But as she became a better rider, she had begun to dream of buying Buck and putting him on the Montana ranch so that no one else could ever ride him.

Wendy swallowed a sob. She remembered

those three long weeks in the hospital after the accident, waiting for the day when she could go to the stable and tell Buck how sorry she was.

On her second day home from the hospital, her father had left for work, telling her to rest. As soon as he was gone, she had gotten dressed to go to the stable. All the way there, she had thought of Buck, picturing him running free in a pasture, growing well and strong again.

"May I help you?" one of the many young stablemen had asked her, she recalled, the picture growing ever more vivid in her mind.

"I was wondering where Buck is," she said, pointing toward his empty stall. "I didn't think he'd be well enough to be ridden yet. Do you know when he'll be back?"

"Buck? Are you kidding?"

Wendy shook her head, puzzled. "The big buckskin with three white feet and a blaze . . . the one that stays in this stall."

"Buck." The man nodded.

"Where is he?"

"He had to be put away. Some crazy kid was showing off and rode him into a pickup truck. Broke both of his front legs. You ever ride him? Didn't hear about it?"

33

The man said more, but Wendy didn't hear it. She was escaping, stumbling painfully on her weak leg, from the memory-haunted stable and the accusingly empty stall. Her father hadn't told her. He hadn't told her that Buck was dead —that she had killed him.

Wendy never told her father about her visit to the stable. She waited every day, dreading the moment he'd talk to her about the accident, but the subject never came up. They discussed the future but never the past.

It wasn't that her father did not care about the horse; he had just wanted her to forget, she told herself. After her mother died, they hadn't talked much about her long illness, and somehow the pain had faded.

Concentrating on that idea, Wendy forced her grief down. She had most of her clothes unpacked and put away by the time a light tap on her door brought her out to supper.

"Are you getting settled?" Aunt Laura asked as she carried a salad and a basket of corn bread to the table.

"I've unpacked enough to know that I brought all the wrong things," Wendy said. "I didn't realize that it was still winter here. I've got a closet full of summer cottons."

"Didn't you bring any sweaters?" her aunt asked.

"A few cardigans. The rest are packed in the boxes Daddy is supposed to send."

"Well, I've got lots of sweaters, so you can wear them till yours get here. They'll be a little large, but at least you'll be warm." Her aunt indicated the chair facing the window, and Wendy sat down.

"It sure smells good," she said.

"One of the reasons we have so many returning guests every year—Laura's food," Uncle Art said. "Once they taste her cooking, they want to come back for more."

"Will you teach me that, too?" Wendy asked. "If I could cook, we wouldn't need a housekeeper when Daddy finally gets back from Europe next year."

After she spoke, Wendy saw the quick hurt look flicker across her aunt's face, and she was sorry. Aunt Laura, however, said, "You'll be learning to cook this summer. I'll need your help when the guests come."

To change the subject, Wendy turned to Uncle Art. "I saw one of your horses," she said.

"You saw what?" He looked surprised.

"Abigail wanted to get out the window, so I opened it, and while I was looking around, a horse came out of the trees." Wendy pointed. "Right over there."

"Are you sure it wasn't a deer—or maybe one of the cattle?" he asked.

Wendy shook her head. "I saw it plainly. A sorrel, about a yearling, I'd say, with a white blaze and high white stockings on the hind legs. It was very pretty." Wendy took another bite of the casserole, then looked back at her uncle. "Why are you surprised?"

"Because there aren't any horses loose in this area. The dude herd is in the south pasture, and all my Appaloosas are in the barn corral. I was just down there feeding them."

"Well, it *was* a horse," Wendy said firmly. "It was looking this way, and then a noise scared it and it ran back into the trees."

Uncle Art sighed. "I guess I'll have to start riding fence tomorrow," he said. "It sure doesn't sound like any horse of mine."

"Oh." Wendy couldn't keep the disappointment out of her voice.

"What's the matter?" her uncle asked.

Wendy forced a smile. "Nothing. I guess I was just sort of hoping that it was yours. It was so pretty." She kept her eyes on her plate, not wanting her aunt and uncle to know that she'd weakened for even a second. She should be grateful that the sorrel didn't belong on the Cross-R. Just seeing it had brought back all her painful memories.

# 3 · Ranch Life

WENDY WAS FEELING quite comfortable with her aunt and uncle by the time she'd finished her supper and the huge wedge of apple pie Aunt Laura served for dessert. Her aunt's and uncle's tales about various guests were funny, and they seemed to accept her as part of the family with an ease she hadn't expected. Wendy followed her uncle's example by stacking her dishes and carrying them to the sink as soon as she had finished eating.

"Would you like me to do the dishes, Aunt Laura?" she asked.

"You sit and talk to me while I rinse them for the dishwasher," her aunt said. "You don't have to help with dishes—not on your first night here, anyway."

"You have a dishwasher?"

Her aunt nodded. "I put my foot down when we started having guests. That's one time our money didn't end up on four feet," she added jokingly.

"Speaking of four-legged creatures, I guess it's too dark to go out to look at the horses tonight," Uncle Art said. "But tomorrow I want to show you my Appaloosas. If there's any horse that can tempt you back to riding, I'm sure it will be one of them."

Wendy smiled and nodded, not trusting herself to speak. Her uncle's words confirmed her fears. He didn't really understand how she felt. He wouldn't try to force her to ride, but he would always be hoping that she'd change her mind about riding.

"As soon as I get these in the dishwasher, I'll show you the rest of the house," Aunt Laura said, seeming to sense the tension.

"I'd like that," Wendy said. "If it's anything like what I've seen so far, it must be a wonderful place to live. I really love my room."

"I'm glad," her aunt said. "I had fun fixing it up for you."

Wendy finished clearing the table, then sat and answered her aunt's questions about Phoenix

39

and the life she had known there. Some of the memories hurt, especially when she spoke of Gretchen, her onetime best friend. But much of it seemed nearly as far away in time as it was in miles. Except for the dull ache in her leg, even the accident might have happened years ago, instead of only weeks.

"Well, that was quick, wasn't it?" her aunt asked, closing the dishwasher door firmly. "Now I'll show you around."

She led the way through the dining room and into the hall again. She passed the door to Wendy's room and opened the next one, to an extra-large bathroom. "This is the guest bath in the summer, when we have groups for dinner and entertainment afterward." She moved on to the final door on the east side. "And this is our room," she said, stepping inside.

"Wow!" Wendy said appreciatively. "You ought to go into interior decorating. This is prettier than the model homes Mom and I used to go and look at."

The room was very large. The floor was covered with an olive tweed rug, and heavy gold, brown, and olive print drapes flanked two wide windows. The same satin material covered the king-sized bed. Twin chairs were done in brown, and there were several gold cushions scattered on the bed. The effect was both beautiful and restful.

"It's rather grand for us," Aunt Laura admitted, "but we spend quite a bit of our time in here when the guests are using the living room." She opened one of the folding closet doors that ran the full length of the inside wall. "We even have our own television set in here."

Wendy laughed. "Sounds like you've got everything all set for summer," she said.

"We've had guests for five years now, so we've learned how to handle it pretty well. They're only here for about three and a half months out of the year, so it isn't long enough for us to get tired of them. I really look forward to each tourist season. I hope you will, too."

"I'm sure I will," Wendy said with more confidence than she felt.

"Now, from the sublime to the ridiculous," Aunt Laura said, crossing the hall to the single door on the west side. "Art claims this door should be padlocked to keep the overflow from toppling out into the rest of the house. But it isn't really that bad."

41

Wendy followed her in, then stopped in surprise. After the neatness of the other rooms, it was somewhat of a shock. The room was a chaos of materials, patterns, boxes, and shelves. A chair, its cloth skin removed and its stuffing neatly boxed beside it, sat to one side, its bare springs gleaming dully. There were several cans of paint and furniture stain on the shelves. The only cleared floor space was around a large sewing machine.

"This is my workroom," Aunt Laura said, laughter in her voice.

"You must be terribly busy," Wendy said, "but it does look interesting."

"Tomorrow is Sunday, but maybe Monday or Tuesday we can run into Littleville and get some material for you—if you really are serious about learning to sew."

"I'm serious," Wendy said emphatically. "Besides, I'm going to need a warmer wardrobe while I'm here, so I may as well try to make it."

"Good girl," Aunt Laura said. "We'll have a lot of fun. You join Art in the living room now, while I give Peg Carter a call and find out when she wants you to start your schooling."

Wendy winced. "Just when I was planning

all kinds of new projects," she wailed.

"I'm sure it won't be too bad," her aunt said. "If you set aside a couple of hours every day, you'll have it all behind you in no time. Most things are just a matter of concentration."

"Right," Wendy agreed. "And I will concentrate, I promise. It means a lot to me to be able to finish the year on my own, without going to a strange school."

"You run on out and keep your uncle company, and I'll see what I can find out," Aunt Laura promised.

Wendy found her way back through the dining room and into the living room. Like the rustic dining room, with its plank tables and oil-lamp-style chandelier, the living room was pure Old West. It was a large, comfortable room containing several chintz-covered couches and chairs. The tables and lamps were of rustic-finished wood, and even the large television set was encased in a knotty pine cabinet. A fire blazed in the big corner fireplace, and Uncle Art looked completely relaxed, stretched out in a chair with the newspaper.

"Well," he said, "think you'll be happy here, Wendy? We hope you'll feel at home."

"It's a terrific place," Wendy said, not sure how to answer the question since it hadn't seemed casually asked. Trying to slip away lightly, she observed, "Your house has a split personality, though."

Uncle Art laughed, but his eyes told her that he'd seen through her ruse. "When a place serves two different purposes, it has to suit them both, I guess. You'll get used to that. You'll soon get used to a lot of things."

"I'll try to get used to everything," Wendy said honestly. "I really do want to be a part of this place and your life here. Before the accident, I used to dream of coming here. That's why I badgered Daddy into letting me take riding lessons. It was something I'd always wanted to do."

Her uncle took his time folding the paper, then leaned forward, his weathered face solemn. "Horses *are* very much a part of this ranch, Wendy," he said. "They do much of the work, as well as being my hobby. You can't really be a part of the way we live here, without coming into contact with them."

Wendy squirmed under his intense gaze. "I know that."

"I'm not saying that you have to ride to live here, because that's not so. All I want you to see is that you will be very limited if you don't."

"I understand that," she said. "But I just don't think I ever want to ride a horse again, not after what happened. I—I get sick every time I even think about getting on a horse."

Uncle Art nodded. "Well," he said, "you've got time, and that's important. The horses will be here for you to try anytime you want to. Shall we leave it at that?"

"Thank you," Wendy said. "I know it's a dumb way to be, but. . . ."

"It isn't really," her uncle reassured her. "You were badly hurt, and you haven't forgotten it. Subconsciously, you don't want to take a chance on its happening again. The trouble is, to fit in with the young people your age around here, you'll almost have to ride. I don't think there's a single pupil in the Littleville school who doesn't ride."

"Oh." Wendy settled herself on the couch to digest that fact. Somehow it hadn't occurred to her that horses would be so important here; in Phoenix, only Gretchen had shared her deep love of horses.

"Well, now, didn't Art show you how to operate the TV?" Aunt Laura asked from the doorway. "I'm afraid that's about all we have to offer in the way of entertainment around here."

"We were talking," Uncle Art said. "Did you get Peg?"

Aunt Laura nodded, turning to Wendy. "She thinks she can be ready for you to start on Monday or Tuesday, after school."

"So soon?" Wendy couldn't keep the disappointment out of her voice.

Aunt Laura laughed as she switched on the television and settled herself in a chair with her knitting. "You'll have a lot more spare time now than you will this summer, so you'd just as well get it over with if you can. Peg said she'd give you a set of tests first, to see exactly where you need help, then work with you to prepare for the final exams. A lot will depend on how far along you were in Phoenix." Aunt Laura spread her knitting out on her knees for a moment, examining the bronze gold yarn.

"What are you making?" Wendy asked.

"A sweater for me," her uncle answered, before her aunt could reply. "Which I need."

46

"Like you need another horse?" Aunt Laura teased him. "Would you like to learn to knit, Wendy?"

"I'd love to, if you're not too busy." Wendy looked questioningly at her uncle.

"Pay no attention to Art," her aunt said. "He has more hand-knit sweaters than anybody in Montana. Our winter evenings are quiet, and I get a lot done. Come on, I'll show you how to cast on the stitches and what to do with them after you get them on the needle."

The evening passed quickly and pleasantly as Wendy worked back and forth on her long, straight swatch of knitting. By the time her uncle announced that he was going to bed, she had knit nearly eight inches. She spread out her work and sighed at the unevenness of the stitches. "Do you think I'll ever be able to knit anything?" she asked her aunt anxiously. "It doesn't look a bit like yours."

"It looks very good for a first try," her aunt assured her. "You've caught on faster than most people do. One more square, and you'll be ready to knit a scarf or maybe some slippers like these." She extended her foot to show bright blue slippers with black soles and cuffs.

"Those are cute," Wendy said, "but they look hard."

"They're really simple—and useful. I wear them every evening from September through May. The floors are always cold." She stuffed the ever-growing sweater into her knitting bag and got up.

"May I get a bid in for a second pair of slippers?" Uncle Art asked. "Mine have holes."

Wendy laughed. "I'll knit them if you'll wear them," she promised.

"If I can get you trained as well as I have Laura, I'll be the best-dressed man around," he said, giving her shoulders a hug before going to turn off the lights. "See you in the morning."

"Good night," Wendy said. "See you tomorrow."

The knitting had made her sleepy, but once she was undressed and snuggled down under several blankets, Wendy's eyes refused to close. The silence that surrounded her seemed louder than the traffic noises at home. Moonlight spilled in through her slightly open window, and she stared up at the bright, twinkling stars, wondering if she could grow used to this way of life.

So far, it had been surprisingly pleasant, and

she could see that it would be easy to love her new life with her aunt and uncle. But it wasn't going to be all evenings by the fireplace, watching television and knitting. There would be schoolwork and guests and horses—always horses.

Wendy sighed, knowing that tomorrow her uncle would insist on introducing her to his prized Appaloosas. It was inevitable.

Suddenly a shadow darkened the patch of moonlight on her bed. Wendy nearly screamed before she recognized Abigail's fuzzy shape.

"Meow?" the cat inquired from the window-sill.

"Come on in," Wendy called softly.

The cat needed no second invitation. In a moment she was curled up beside Wendy, her delighted purr filling the silence and lulling Wendy to sleep.

# 4 · Mismatch

THE SHARP SCENT of frying bacon woke Wendy early the next morning. Abigail was gone, and Wendy shivered as she hurried to close the window. She thought longingly of the floor-length flannel nightgowns she had seen in the stores last winter. Maybe she could start her sewing by making one, she thought, dressing in her warmest slacks and blouse and her heaviest cardigan.

Full of such plans, Wendy started for the door, only to be halted by a plaintive whinny. Curious, she went to her window and looked across the meadow to the trees. The horse was there again, its coat shiny red against the dark forest. There were answering whinnies from the stables on the other side of the house, then the quick sound of hoofbeats. The sorrel vanished

51

into the trees like a phantom, just before a rider came loping into view. Uncle Art reined in the big Appaloosa he was riding, looked around for a moment, then shrugged and disappeared back around the corner of the house.

Wendy watched the trees for several more minutes but saw nothing. Hunger spurring her, she gave her long hair a quick brushing and hurried out to the kitchen.

Her aunt looked up with a smile. "I thought I heard you. Help yourself." She gestured toward the waiting family-style breakfast.

Wendy picked up a plate and began filling it with bacon, scrambled eggs, and toast from the heated serving dishes. "Has Uncle Art eaten?" she asked.

"No, he's busy with the horses. He'll be here in a minute, I think."

"I saw him riding a big Appaloosa," Wendy said.

"That's his prize stallion, Happy Warrior. He was using him to round up the mares and the young stock."

"Round them up? I thought they were in the corrals." Wendy noticed that her aunt looked disturbed. "Did something happen?"

52

"We're not quite sure," Aunt Laura said, handing Wendy a glass of milk before sitting down with her own plate of food. "When he went out to feed the stock this morning, the corral gate was open, and the mares were wandering around loose."

Before Wendy could ask any more questions, the back door opened, and her uncle came in. "Did you find them all?" Aunt Laura asked quickly.

He nodded, then called good morning to Wendy. "They were all right around here. It looked as if they just got out by accident."

"Could you have left the gate unlatched last night?" Aunt Laura asked as she served up her husband's breakfast and poured coffee for him and for herself.

"I'd hate to think I'm getting that absent-minded," he said, "but I can't figure it out. There was no one around, as far as I could see, and with all the horses accounted for, it can't have been a thief." He took a sip of coffee, then turned to Wendy. "And how are you this morning?" he asked. "Ready for an outdoor tour?"

"If someone has a jacket I can borrow," Wendy said. "My room felt like the North Pole."

"I've got several," Aunt Laura said. "You can see which one fits best."

After a moment, Wendy asked, "Did you see it this time?"

"See what?" her uncle asked.

"The sorrel. It was standing by the woods, whinnying, just before you rode around the house."

"So that's who was calling the horses," he said. "I thought I was hearing things. I had all my horses in, but I rode around to look, anyway. It must have dodged back before I got there."

"At least now you know that it isn't a deer," Wendy teased.

Her uncle laughed, then sobered. "I guess I'll have to spend the morning riding fence. I sure don't want any of my cattle out on the roads somewhere."

Aunt Laura sighed. "Things like this always seem to happen when Cliff and George aren't here to help."

"I'll just check the north and east fences today," Uncle Art said. "They're closest to any danger areas."

"Could I—uh—walk part of it?" Wendy asked. She noticed a fleeting, though unmistakable,

54

look of disappointment on her uncle's face when she said "walk." It was obvious to Wendy that he had hoped she would ride with him.

"It's rough territory," Aunt Laura said, "and you're not familiar with it."

"If I'm following the fence line, I can't get lost," Wendy said. "And I am supposed to get a lot of exercise."

"If Wendy could check the north end as far east as the stream, it would help," her aunt said quickly, glancing at her husband. "She can follow the stream back; it won't be too far."

Her uncle nodded slowly. "We'll start right after breakfast," he said finally. "You follow the fence, on foot, from the far side of Happy's paddock. We can take a quick look at the horses before you go, all right?"

"All right." Wendy was glad that he'd accepted her offer without too much fuss.

The sun had warmed the air a little by the time she and her uncle walked out the front door and followed the rock-edged path through the meadow to the first corral.

"Were the cattle loose, too?" Wendy asked as their red and white heads and dark, gentle eyes turned her way curiously.

"Nope. Just the horses." Her uncle slid between the corral bars and walked across the first big corral to the next, where seventeen horses stood watching. "This is the corral that was open."

Wendy paused at the fence and stared appreciatively at the horses beyond. There were four older mares with foals at their sides, five yearlings, and four young horses in the corral. All were dark brown or black, with the Appaloosa white blanket across their shoulders or haunches. "They're beauties," she said at last, conscious of her uncle's gaze.

"These are the best I've raised," he said proudly. "I've got two more mares in the barn, waiting to foal. The yearlings are last year's foals. The three over there are the two-year-olds I'm breaking to sell, and that one dark filly on the far side is a three-year-old that I'm thinking of keeping."

"I don't know how you could bear to sell any of them." The words were out before Wendy could stop them, and she felt a blush spreading over her face. "I mean, if I'd raised a horse from the time it was a foal, I'd worry about its having someone who really cared—"

56

"Would you like one of them?" her uncle asked.

"What do you mean?"

"I mean, would you like to have one of the foals or a yearling for your own?"

"To take care of?" Wendy asked.

"No. To own. To raise and train and love, the way I've raised and trained and loved them." His eyes met hers, and Wendy realized his words were a challenge as well as an offer.

One of the mares came to sniff her arm, and Wendy tensed. "I don't think I could," she said at last. "I'm only going to be here for a year, Uncle Art. It wouldn't be fair to you or the horse, would it?"

Her uncle nodded slowly. "What do you say we just let the offer stand for a while?" he asked. "You can help me halterbreak all of them, and maybe by the time we're through, you'll be more certain of how you feel about things. Besides, there are two more foals still to be born. You really ought to see them all before you make any decisions."

"Thank you," Wendy said, hoping he'd realize that it was for the way he seemed to understand as well as for his offer. She followed him into

57

the corral, not too frightened by the way the horses crowded around. After a moment she was cautiously petting or scratching their broad foreheads.

"Well, I guess we'd better get going on those fences," her uncle said after a few minutes. "Come on. I'll introduce you to Happy."

Wendy followed him into the next pen, which was longer and narrower than the two corrals. A stream crossed the lower end of it, and when her uncle whistled, the saddled black and white horse that was grazing near it came trotting toward them, stirrups bouncing against his sides. Wendy recognized him immediately as the horse her uncle had been riding earlier.

"This is Happy Warrior," Uncle Art said proudly, "the finest Appaloosa I've ever owned. Isn't he a beauty? If any of those new foals turn out to be like him, I'm going to retire from dude ranching and just raise horses."

Wendy struggled to keep from retreating. The stallion was big and powerful-looking, his muscles rippling under the black-spotted white blanket on his haunches. Just the fact that he was saddled made him seem different from the other horses—frightening.

"Is that the way I'm supposed to go?" she asked, deliberately turning toward the far end of the pasture.

"You start at the corner of Happy's pasture and follow the fence that way. I'll go the other way. You just go as far as you want to. If you don't get to the stream, don't worry about it. I can check the rest this afternoon."

"What if I find the broken fence?" Wendy asked, making her way toward the end of the pasture.

"Try to block the opening if you can," her uncle said as he mounted. "If you can't, come back and tell Laura. She can drive the pickup out and use that to block it if I'm not back. All I'm worried about is losing stock on the highway."

Wendy shuddered at the memory of what could happen to an animal on a highway. She heard her uncle talking to the stallion but didn't look back as he rode out. She stepped across the narrow stream, slid between the paddock bars, and set off along the barbed-wire fence. It was, she told herself, a lovely day for a hike.

The air soon warmed enough for her to shed the jacket, then her cardigan. Occasionally she

59

caught glimpses of the cows and calves. She found her eyes repeatedly roving away from the fence and realized, rather surprisingly, that it was in hope of spotting the mysterious sorrel.

The splashing of the stream told her when she was nearly at the end of her section of fence. She had seen no sign of the horse. The stream wandered in under the fence and drifted away from it at an angle. Wendy, growing weary, followed it into the woods.

She had lost sight of the fence when she heard the snorting of a horse. Could it be her uncle already? she wondered, hurrying ahead, eager to report that the fence in her section was unbroken. She rounded a bend of the stream and nearly ran broadside into a cow. Startled, Wendy stumbled back, but the cow paid no attention to her.

Two sounds came from the brush beyond the cow—a calf's bleat and the whinny of a terrified horse. The cow started forward, head down, tail twisted up in anger. Not knowing what to expect, Wendy shouted, "Watch out!"

The cow hesitated, seeming to notice Wendy for the first time. Wendy took full advantage of the animal's confusion, grabbing a stick and forcing the cow away from the brush. That accomplished, she hurried around the thick, thorny growth to see what was causing the trouble.

Two animals stared at her in wide-eyed terror. Wendy ran first to the smallest—a calf, not more than a day or two old. His problem seemed easily solved. He'd fallen into a small but deep gash in the ground, landing on his back, with all four legs in the air. He hadn't been able to get out, and his cries were driving his worried mother to attack.

The calf proved surprisingly heavy, but Wendy managed to tug and boost him out of the gully and back up onto his shaky legs. Still bleating piteously, he stumbled to where his mother stood pawing the ground, ready to renew her attack.

Wendy turned to the second animal. "Well, now, what are you doing here?" she asked the blaze-faced sorrel. "How did you manage to get between a cow and her calf?"

The horse shivered and tried to back away from her, then whimpered in pain. Wendy looked down and saw that the filly's front legs were caught in some loose barbed wire.

61

Her first impulse was to run to the little horse and tear at the awful wire, but Wendy controlled herself. The filly was frightened; if she struggled against the wire, she'd cut herself up badly.

"Steady now . . . it's going to be all right," Wendy said, not moving. "I won't hurt you, I promise. I just want to help."

The filly calmed down and flicked her ears forward to listen. Wendy could see that she was almost perfect, her only obvious flaw being that she had one blue eye and one brown one. Slim, as lightly built as a deer, with dainty legs and a small, graceful head, she was certainly no ordinary wild horse. Signs of careful breeding were plain in the filly's impressive lines. She was beautiful.

"Will you let me touch you?" Wendy asked, taking a careful step forward. "How about it, little gypsy horse—will you let me help you? You can't get free by yourself. You'll have to let me help."

The filly's skin quivered under her fingers, but she seemed to understand Wendy's words. She didn't struggle or try to move away. Wendy took her time, talking to the filly soothingly

62

and petting her for several minutes before trying to touch the wire.

The coil was wrapped cruelly about the horse's slender legs, and when Wendy touched it, the filly jumped, digging the barbs in deeper. Wendy stood up and again stroked the trembling horse to calm her. She couldn't leave and go for help; by the time she returned, the filly might have killed herself trying to escape the wire's grip.

Wendy looked around and saw her cardigan lying on the ground, where she'd dropped it. Would a blindfold help? she wondered. There seemed to be nothing else she could try. Talking softly, she got the cardigan and, taking plenty of time, eased it up around the filly's neck, then down over the delicate ears and big eyes. Wondering if she was doing the right thing, she secured it by tying the sweater arms together.

For a moment Wendy thought the filly was going to fight, but the sudden darkness seemed to freeze the horse, and Wendy didn't wait for the spell to wear off. As gently as she could, she began unwinding the wire. More than once as she pulled the barbs from the filly's flesh, she ended up with them embedded in her own. By the time the last of the wire was uncoiled, Wendy was trembling as violently as the filly.

"What in the world?" The sound of her uncle's voice brought Wendy's trembling under control.

"She was caught in the wire. Watch out—it's right over there," Wendy warned.

The filly shied, nearly knocking Wendy down, as she heard the new voice. Wendy threw her arms around the horse's neck and held on.

"Hold her," Uncle Art said. "I've got a rope." He dismounted and uncoiled the rope from his saddle.

"She's awfully frightened," Wendy said. "Let me put the rope on her. Get the wire so that none of the other animals will be caught."

Her uncle handed her the rope and began carefully gathering together the loose wire. Wendy waited until the filly stopped trembling, then, leaving her blindfolded, knotted the rope into a halter and secured it in place. Gently she removed the sweater.

"Well, little gypsy," Wendy said, "are you ready to go home with me?"

As if in answer, the filly took a limping step, her mismatched eyes no longer white-ringed with fear. Wendy slipped an arm over the filly's neck to guide her, instead of depending on the rope. They both limped a little, and as she walked beside the filly, Wendy was almost glad that the horse was a stray and would soon be taken away. If she stayed, it would be impossible not to love her.

# 5 · *Found and Lost*

WHEN SHE REACHED the ranch, Wendy found
the barn door open. Uncle Art had ridden ahead
to prepare one of the vacant stalls with freshly
spread straw on the floor, water in the bucket,
and hay in the rack.

"Well, you certainly aren't wild, are you, little
gypsy?" Wendy said as the filly, without hesita-
tion, followed her into the stall. "You know what
barns and stalls are for."

Wendy closed the stall door behind them,
smiling at the way the filly went right over to
check the feedbox. "You can have some oats in
a minute," she said, running her hand over the
rib-ridged side. "You look as though you've
missed a few meals."

"I'll bring the oats," her uncle said, stepping
out of the tack room at the far end of the barn.

"That'll help her to accept me."

"Isn't she a beauty?" Wendy asked. "I hope the wire didn't cut her up too badly."

"I'll check as soon as we make friends," Uncle Art said, advancing along the wide aisle between the two rows of stalls, carrying a bucket of oats.

"Easy, Gypsy," Wendy said. "He won't hurt you, girl. He's bringing you something to eat."

The thin filly didn't seem to hear her words. She was shaking; her ears were back tight against her head. She turned, presenting her haunches to the doorway—obviously prepared to kick. Uncle Art stopped and shook his head. "I guess she's not ready for an introduction just yet," he said. "You'd better come and get the oats."

"What about her legs?" Wendy asked.

"You'll have to take care of them. I've got medicated salve that will disinfect them and help the healing. It'll be easier on her if you can wash the cuts and rub salve on them without a battle, but I can throw and tie her if need be."

Wendy shook her head. "She trusts me," she said. "She didn't even make a fuss when I pulled the barbs out of her legs."

"I'll get some warm water and the salve, then

stay out of the way while you work on her."

Gypsy was soon busy eating and didn't notice when Uncle Art approached the stall and handed Wendy the bucket and salve. She knelt down in the straw after wetting a rag and began gently to dab the dried blood from the horse's legs. Carefully washing both front legs from fetlock to shoulder, Wendy was sure she didn't miss any of the cuts and scratches.

The filly stopped eating several times and put her head down to sniff at Wendy; then, apparently satisfied, she resumed her munching of the oats. She winced when Wendy touched the cuts, but she showed no signs of fighting or of trying to escape. Wendy's back and shoulders ached from the strain, and when she finally straightened up, she could hardly stand on her leg.

"You look worse than she does," Uncle Art said from the shadows. "Are you through?"

"I guess so," Wendy said, leaning on the filly for support.

"She'll be all right. You get up to the house. Laura's had dinner ready for half an hour, and I think we're expecting company this afternoon."

"Let me get the rope off, and I'll be right

there," Wendy said, realizing that it had been hours since breakfast.

"I'll check the tack room for a web halter that'll fit her." Uncle Art disappeared, then returned with a lightweight halter. As he neared the stall, Gypsy backed into the far corner, facing him with ears back and teeth bared.

"I don't know what's the matter with her," Wendy said, reaching out for the halter.

"You'd better go a little slow—" her uncle began, but Wendy was already slipping the halter over the delicate nostrils and buckling it in place. The filly made no move to escape Wendy's touch.

"You be good now, Gypsy," Wendy said, giving the arched neck a final pat. "I'll be back to see you after dinner." As she joined her uncle at the barn door, Wendy asked, "What do you think of her? Isn't she pretty?"

"That she is, but she's an odd one, too. I have no idea who might own her."

"Really?" Wendy slowed a little. "I thought she must be a stray from nearby."

Uncle Art shook his head. "I've never seen her before. She's a nice-looking animal; probably a purebred Morgan or half-Arab. I'll have to call the sheriff and see if any horse like that has been reported missing."

"Will she stay here till you find her owner?" Wendy asked, not sure what she wanted his answer to be.

"I suppose so." They walked in silence to the back door of the house. "By the way," Uncle Art asked, "did you find the break in the fence?"

Wendy shook her head. "I didn't find anything except Gypsy—and a calf stuck in the mud. The fence is fine all the way to the stream. Didn't you find it?"

"No, I didn't."

"Well, how did Gypsy get here?" Wendy asked.

Uncle Art shrugged. "Maybe there's a fence down in one of the other pastures. I don't know how she'd get from them over here, though. I guess I'll have to check every foot of fence on the place."

"I wish she weren't so scared of you," Wendy said. "I'd like to have you take a closer look at her legs. I don't know anything about giving first aid to a horse."

"Well, maybe after dinner you can get Laura to look at her. She's good at doctoring, and the

71

filly may accept a woman more easily— especially if she's been hurt or frightened by a man. But right now, I think *you* could use a little first aid."

Wendy followed his gaze to her hands and agreed. There were dozens of gouges and cuts, where she'd caught them in the barbed wire. "I did have some trouble getting the wire loose," she admitted.

"I'm surprised the filly stood still for it, skittish as she is. Even blindfolded, there are a lot of horses who'd tear themselves apart trying to get away."

"She seemed to know that I was going to help her," Wendy said.

"I'll call the sheriff while you get those cuts cleaned up," her uncle said, opening the back door for her. "Laura, get the first aid kit!"

Wendy told about finding and freeing the filly, while her aunt attended to the cuts on Wendy's hands and arms. But even as Wendy talked, her thoughts were on the phone call her uncle was making. She hurried out to the hall the moment Aunt Laura had finished. "What did he say?" she asked.

"Not much, Wendy. He hasn't had any reports of a yearling filly missing, but it could be that her owner doesn't even know she's gone yet. He's going to call around to some of the ranchers and see if any of them owns a filly with one blue eye and one brown."

"Then—she'll be staying here?" Wendy asked, not sure whether to feel glad or sorry about the news.

Uncle Art nodded. "I really should call the vet to check those cuts," he said. "I'd hate to have to rough her up, but an infection could be bad."

Wendy hesitated, then said, "She seems so scared of you—she might get hurt worse fighting if you touch her."

"Let's talk about this over dinner," Aunt Laura said. "Peg and Carol will be here in an hour, and I'd like to get the dishes out of the way before they come."

Wendy blinked at her aunt for a moment, wondering why she was looking at her so expectantly, then remembered that Peg Carter was to be her teacher. "Who is Carol?" she asked.

"Peg's daughter. She's your age and very anxious to meet you. They live on the next ranch, so you and Carol will probably see a lot of each other."

73

"That's nice," Wendy said absently. "Will you have time to go out and see Gypsy before they come?" she asked.

"I think it might be a good idea for you to check the cuts, Laura," Uncle Art said. "You'll know whether or not we need a vet."

"I think it might help to let Peg and Carol see her, too," Aunt Laura suggested. "If there's anyone around who'll recognize the filly, it's Carol. She knows every horse in this part of the state."

"I don't think that girl ever thinks of anything but horses, does she?" Uncle Art asked with a laugh. Wendy forced an uneasy smile.

Dinner was quickly served and eaten, and Wendy had time to change clothes before a car drove up. The woman who got out was slim and attractive, but Wendy paid more attention to the dark-haired girl beside her. Carol Carter looked as though she belonged on a ranch, around horses, and Wendy was uncomfortable even before they were introduced.

Wendy talked briefly with Mrs. Carter, making a Tuesday appointment for the first tests. Then she was faced with the problem of getting acquainted with Carol.

Uncle Art tried to help by saying, "Wendy, why don't you take Carol down to the barn and see if she recognizes the filly?"

"What filly is that, Mr. Roush?" Carol asked quickly, her face lighting up with interest.

"A little stray that Wendy found this morning." There was obvious pride in Uncle Art's voice. "She was tangled in some loose barbed wire, and Wendy had to untangle her. The sheriff doesn't have any record of her being missing, so I'm keeping her here while he tries to locate her owner."

"You got her out of barbed wire?" Carol looked at Wendy with more interest.

Wendy nodded. "She was so good—even when it hurt her, she didn't try to fight."

"That's unusual," Carol said. "Most horses panic and cut themselves up fighting the wire."

"She's really a beauty," Wendy went on, but then she paused. Carol reminded her of Gretchen—the way she herself had been before the accident. She and Gretchen had spent most of their time together riding or talking of horses. But after Buck's death, Gretchen wasn't friendly anymore. Carol wouldn't want to be friends, either, if she knew—

"What is she? I mean, quarter horse, Appaloosa, what?" Carol moved quickly toward the door.

"Uncle Art said she might be a purebred Morgan or half-Arab." Wendy almost had to run to keep up with Carol. "She's awfully shy, though. She wouldn't even let Uncle Art get near her."

Wendy felt a touch of anger at the way Carol hurried through the half-open barn door and switched on the overhead lights. "Which stall is she in?" she asked.

"You'd better let me go first," Wendy said, moving ahead of the slightly taller brunette. "We don't want to—" She stopped to stare at the open stall door. "She's gone!" she gasped.

"What?" Carol came to stand beside her. "Are you sure she isn't in one of the other stalls?" She moved on along the row of stalls, looking over the doors.

Wendy didn't say anything. She was trying to remember if she'd closed the stall door properly. She was sure she remembered sliding the wooden bar into place before she'd hung the bloodstained rag in the next stall to dry. But if she'd closed the stall securely, where was Gypsy?

## 6 · Misfit

SHE'S NOT in any of the other stalls," Carol said, coming back to stand beside Wendy. "Do you think you left the door loose?"

Wendy shook her head. "I remember sliding the bar tight. I checked it specially, because we left the barn door open, and I didn't want her getting out."

Carol closed the stall door, then slid the bar across. "If you closed it tight, I don't see how she got out," she said.

"I don't either. Someone must have turned her loose, but. . . ." Wendy let her words trail off, realizing that there was no one else around.

Carol shrugged. "Tell your uncle we'll take a couple of the horses out and find her. She should be around pretty close."

"You mean—ride out and look for her?"

Wendy felt her stomach tightening.

"Don't you want to find her?" Carol asked in a surprised tone.

"I can't ride just yet," Wendy began. "I was in this accident and broke my leg and—"

"Your aunt told me, but I thought she said you were well. How did you find the filly in the first place if you weren't riding?"

"I was out walking along the fence, checking it for breaks and—" Wendy could see the growing doubt in the other girl's eyes. She hated herself for lying about her injury, but she knew that this girl, who was so sure of herself around horses, would never understand. "Anyway, I don't think we could find her on horseback. Even Uncle Art couldn't get close to her."

Carol shrugged. "Well, she won't go far on sore legs. She'll probably come back for dinner. Let's go look at the foals," she said. "I've got my eye on one of your uncle's yearlings, and he's promised to give me first chance if he decides to sell her."

"Which one is that?" Wendy asked, trying to sound interested. She longed to walk back into the woods alone, sure that Gypsy would come back to her if she did.

"The black one on the far side; the one with the little star and the shoulder blanket. Isn't she a beauty? I want her for a gymkhana horse. That smallest mare on the end is her mother, so I'm hoping this filly will stay small. I think a gymkhana horse should be a little shorter than a regular horse, don't you?"

Wendy sighed. "I don't even know what a gymkhana horse is," she admitted. "I've heard of gymkhanas, but I've never seen one."

Carol smiled. "Gymkhana horses are specially trained for the kind of contests we have in gymkhanas. They have to be quick and sure-footed for barrel-racing and pole-bending and other events." She paused, then went on, her voice inviting friendship. "We have gymkhanas every summer. You'll have to come to our practices so you can learn to ride in them with the rest of us."

Once again Wendy's stomach tightened at the mention of riding. "I don't think so," she said unenthusiastically. "I'm supposed to help Aunt Laura with the guests in the summer, so I probably won't—"

"If you don't ride in the gymkhanas, or at least go on our Saddle Club rides, you might as

79

well forget about getting to know anybody," Carol said. "Littleville is a small town, and everybody goes to the gymkhanas—even the guests at this ranch."

"Oh." Wendy leaned on the fence. Mares and young horses crowded up to her, but her mind wasn't on them. She was thinking of the long, lonely months ahead.

If what Carol was saying was true, Wendy was going to be an outcast here, a misfit, because she couldn't ride. She tried to remind herself that it would only be a year—that it would be too painful to make new friends and then leave—and besides, when they found out about Buck. . . .

"I don't see why you can't ride," Carol said. "I mean, if you can walk well enough to check the fence, you should be able to stay on a horse. Kirk broke his leg a couple of years ago, and he even rode with the cast on!"

Wendy was trying to think of something to say, when the honking of a car horn saved her. "That's Mom," Carol said. She smiled. "I'm glad you're here, Wendy. I hope you'll ride over to our place when you can. It's not too far from here, along the beach."

"Thanks a lot," Wendy replied, recognizing

the offer of friendship even though she knew she couldn't accept it. She was sure Carol would withdraw the offer as soon as she learned about Buck.

"Hope you find the filly," Carol called, running ahead to meet her mother at the end of the drive. She waved gaily as they drove away.

Wendy walked slowly up the drive and into the house. Aunt Laura had vanished, but Uncle Art was sitting in his chair. "Did Carol recognize the filly?" he asked.

"She's gone," Wendy said, feeling miserable. "I must have left the door loose. She ran away."

"What?" He laid down the magazine he'd been looking at. "You mean she got out?"

Wendy nodded. "The stall door was open, and we left the barn door unlocked, so it was easy for her to get away."

Uncle Art sighed. "I suppose there's no use in my riding out after her," he said. "The way she acted, she'd just hide from me."

"I could go walking along the stream," Wendy said, though her leg ached already. "Maybe she'd come to me."

Uncle Art looked at her for a moment, then shook his head. "You look too beat. She'll be all right out there. She may just decide to come back on her own—horses don't like being alone, you know, and there are plenty of horses in the corral to attract her. That's probably why she's been hanging around, anyway."

"But what if she gets into more wire?" Wendy asked. "It would be my fault if anything happened to her. It was my carelessness that let her get out."

"I don't think so," Uncle Art said. "She could have worked the gate loose by herself. I've had a few horses that did that just by bouncing the door back and forth. She'll turn up, I'm sure."

"Who'll turn up?" Aunt Laura asked, coming into the room with a box of patterns.

Wendy and her uncle explained about the filly, and Aunt Laura nodded her agreement with Uncle Art's words. "She'll be back, Wendy. She knows where the oats and the other horses are. In fact, if you go down and wait in the barn this evening at feeding time, I'll bet you'll find her there, waiting for some oats."

"Do you really think so?" Wendy asked.

Aunt Laura nodded. "Horses are creatures of habit, and I'd be willing to bet she's been stable raised. That means feeding both morning and night. Just leave the barn door open, and wait out of sight for a while. I think it's worth a try, don't you, Art?"

Uncle Art laughed. "Leave it to you," he said, giving his wife a hug. "It just might work. If not, you can go out with a bucket of oats in the morning. She'll be hungry enough to come to you by then."

"I did some sewing for one of Art's nieces last year," Aunt Laura said, changing the subject, "and I still have the patterns. I thought you might like to look them over and see if there's anything you like. I have some material, too. Nothing fancy, but you can have any of it you want."

For a moment Wendy wavered, her thoughts still on the filly and her desire to find her; then she surrendered to the assurances that her aunt and uncle had offered. In a few minutes she was in the crowded workroom with her aunt, busily sorting through patterns and fabrics, her mind caught by the prospect of new clothes.

"Did you like Carol?" her aunt asked as she and Wendy began cutting a simple jumper from some dark blue corduroy.

"She seems nice," Wendy said, "but I don't

think she'll have much time for being friends with me."

"Why on earth not?" Aunt Laura asked. "She was excited when I told her you were going to stay with us. I know she's lonesome, living out on the farm the way she does."

"She has her horses." Wendy couldn't quite keep the bitterness out of her voice.

"You used to love horses, too," Aunt Laura reminded her.

"But she loves riding them." Wendy's words hung heavy in the air.

"Give yourself time," her aunt said with an understanding smile. "It's only in Western movies that the good guys jump right back in the saddle after a fall. When you're ready to ride again, it'll come naturally; you'll see."

"My pink cardigan should look okay under this, don't you think?" Wendy asked, deliberately changing the subject.

"Perfect. Shall we try to get the jumper done for you to wear to take your tests Tuesday?"

"Do you think we could?"

"Sure. It's a simple pattern, and I have thread and a zipper for it, and, I think, everything else we need."

85

The first seams had already given shape to the jumper by the time a light tap on the door brought Wendy's attention back to other things. "Isn't anyone in there ever going to get hungry?" Uncle Art inquired pitifully as he opened the door.

"I'm sorry, dear," Aunt Laura said. "I didn't realize how late it's getting. I'll go make some sandwiches from that leftover roast. Do you want me to warm the gravy and make hot roast beef sandwiches?"

"Sounds good to me," Uncle Art said. He turned to Wendy. "We can feed the horses as soon as we finish eating."

"You haven't seen Gypsy, have you?" she asked.

He shook his head. "I spent most of the afternoon down at the corral, and there wasn't a sign of her. She may have wandered back the way she came, Wendy."

Wendy didn't argue, but deep down she hoped it wasn't true.

After supper, Aunt Laura got a heavy wool sweater for Wendy to wear under her jacket, and though she felt a little like a sausage in a too-tight casing, Wendy was grateful for the extra warmth as the cold night wind chased her about the corrals.

Uncle Art separated the young horses in the corral from the mares and foals, which he put in the barn for feeding. Wendy hurried back and forth, carrying heavy buckets of oats for each horse, while her uncle forked hay into a dozen big piles.

The young horses were greedy, and the colts crowded out the fillies with squeals of warning. It was easier filling the feedboxes in the individual stalls, and Wendy took her time, leaning over the stall doors to watch as the tiny foals nursed while their mothers ate oats.

Uncle Art finished pitching hay to the barn horses and came to stand beside her. "I'm going up to the house now, but I'll leave the barn door open about halfway. You fill Gypsy's feedbox and leave her stall door open. I'll come back before it gets too late, and if she isn't here by then, you can figure she's gone too far to come back tonight."

Wendy followed her uncle's directions, then settled herself to wait in the shadows. The barn was warmer than the outside, but the half-open door let in a lot of cold air that made her shiver.

Wendy was lonesome now, and her thoughts weren't very good company. She kept remembering what Carol had said about everybody riding in the gymkhanas. Would she ever get through the year? Wendy asked herself. And after a year—then what?

A soft sound brought her attention back to the present. A slender head poked through the open barn door. One blue eye and one brown eye looked around carefully, then the filly limped in and headed for her stall. Wendy waited till she was inside, eating, then she carefully closed the barn door.

"So you did come back, Gypsy," she said.

Gypsy looked around at her calmly enough, then turned her attention back to the oats. Wendy went into the stall, closing the door carefully behind her. "I'm glad you came back," she said, uneasy that she should feel such relief and happiness over the horse's return.

The filly thrust her soft nose against Wendy's chest, whiffling softly through her nostrils. Wendy finger-combed the tangled forelock and scratched behind the small ears. She was still standing that way when Uncle Art came in and switched on the lights.

"I see she came back," he said, not approaching too closely.

"Aunt Laura was right about her coming for food," Wendy said, smiling.

"Well, make sure you close the door firmly this time," he said. "Then come on up to the house. Laura's got a surprise for you."

Wendy gave the filly a good-night pat, then went out, stopping to double-check the stall door before she followed Uncle Art out into the cold night air. "What kind of surprise?" she asked.

"Wait and see," her uncle said with a sly smile.

# 7 · The Only One

AUNT LAURA MET THEM at the door. "Come this way," she said, "but be quiet."

Mystified, Wendy followed her through the house to her own room. The light was on, and there was a small pile of sweaters on the bed. "I brought those in for you to try," Aunt Laura said, "and look what I found."

Wendy followed her aunt's pointing finger to the corner of the room where she'd left her empty suitcases. One was neatly closed, but the other still had a couple of old outfits in it and was open. From inside came soft noises. When she knelt down, Wendy saw Abigail lying on the red and white striped material, with three tiny black kittens snuggled against her.

"If you don't have anything in there you want, I'd like to leave them for a day or two,"

Aunt Laura said. "Abigail's a good mother, and she doesn't like her babies disturbed. If I move them, she's liable to hide them."

"They can stay as long as they want," Wendy said, longing to touch them but holding back because of the way Abigail was watching her. "They're so tiny."

"They'll grow fast enough," Uncle Art said. "In a day or so we'll be able to really look them over, and you can pick one for your own if you like."

Wendy stayed beside the suitcase for nearly an hour, watching as Abigail washed and fussed with her babies. Finally, Aunt Laura called her to the sewing room to work on her jumper again. As they worked, they planned their shopping trip in Littleville.

"We can go in right after lunch Tuesday," Aunt Laura said. "That will give us plenty of time to pick out patterns and material before you have to go to the school at four. Littleville doesn't have many stores, you know—nothing like what you must have had in Phoenix."

Wendy grinned. "Phoenix has lots of stores, but I never had anyone to teach me to knit or sew. And I certainly never had kittens born in my suitcase there." She hesitated, then added, "I didn't have a filly to take care of, either."

Her aunt's smile took on a worried tinge. "Try not to get too attached to her, Wendy," she said. "She must belong to *someone*, and they will be wanting her back."

"Don't worry," Wendy said firmly. "I learned my lesson with Buck. Gypsy is just a little filly that needs my help for a while; that's all."

"Aren't you going to do any more knitting?" Uncle Art asked from the sewing room doorway.

"Lonesome?" Aunt Laura asked.

He grinned at them. "I might as well clear out one end of this room and move my chair in here," he said. "Otherwise I'll spend half my time watching TV alone."

"As soon as we get the facings trimmed and pressed, Wendy can do some hand sewing, and we'll come in and keep you company," Aunt Laura said.

"I'm going to wear this on Tuesday if I get it finished," Wendy said, holding up the nearly completed jumper. "Isn't it pretty?"

"You and Laura will be the fashion plates of old Littleville," he said. "But that's not going to get any slippers knit for me."

"I'll get them done, too," Wendy promised with a smile.

By bedtime the jumper was finished, except for the hem, and Wendy modeled it proudly, trying on first one then another of the sweaters her aunt had brought in. A few were too big, but others fit well and were wonderful to ward off the chill from the window left open slightly for Abigail. Though it was only her first full day on the ranch, Wendy was surprised to discover how much at home she felt as she undressed and climbed into bed.

Looking up at the stars, she almost regretted feeling so comfortable here. How would she feel when she had to leave? If she cared too much for Aunt Laura and Uncle Art, it would be all the more painful when she had to say good-bye.

But how could she not care? Wendy asked herself. They were so good and kind, and she was already involved in so many things. Every hour brought more plans and ideas—from slippers she'd promised to knit to Uncle Art's offer of a foal of her own. And there was Gypsy.

Wendy squirmed and turned away from the window, trying to shut out the pictures that filled her mind. She kept seeing the injured filly.

93

Gypsy needed her, was afraid without her. It was a responsibility Wendy wasn't sure she could deal with. And the more she became involved, the more she would hurt later.

Morning came with cold suddenness. Abigail pounced onto the bed, meowing enthusiastically, and Wendy sat up, rubbing her eyes. From the paleness of the sky outside her window, she knew it wasn't much past dawn. The house was silent. "What's your problem, cat?" she asked.

Abigail hurried toward the suitcase, still meowing. Wendy followed her, shrugging into her heavy robe. A quick inspection showed the kittens curled up together and looking quite all right. Abigail was fussing about the two polished dishes that Aunt Laura had set beside the suitcase. "Meow," she said, meaning *They're empty!*

"You really like an early breakfast, don't you?" Wendy said, yawning. "Well, I guess with your babies to take care of, you need it." She stroked the cat for a moment, then picked up the dishes. "Try not to starve while I'm gone," she said. Abigail, satisfied that action was under way, hopped into the suitcase to check on her babies.

Remembering what her aunt had told her of the morning routine, Wendy plugged in the coffeepot and set out a can of frozen orange juice so it would be thawed enough to mix when the rest of the family got up. Then she filled one of Abigail's dishes with milk and the other with the scraps of roast Aunt Laura had saved especially for the cat.

Watching the kittens while Abigail ate helped Wendy to wake up completely. Keeping as quiet as possible, she got dressed. Her thoughts were on Gypsy as she headed for the kitchen, sure that there would be time before breakfast to check on the filly. Before she reached the back door, however, it banged open, and two men came in.

"Boss!" the taller of the men shouted. "Art?"

"He's still asleep," Wendy said, startled. She realized that these two men must be the ranch hands her uncle had mentioned. "I'm Wendy McLyon," she added. "What's wrong?"

The shorter man stepped forward. "I'm Cliff Harris, and this is George Trent. Do you know anything about the boss keeping a loose horse in the barn?"

"What loose horse?" Uncle Art appeared in the hall, pulling on his robe.

95

"Little sorrel," George said. "When I opened the barn door this morning, it went by me like a freight train."

"Gypsy!" Wendy gasped. "Where is she?"

Cliff shrugged. "She your horse, miss?"

"She's a stray that Wendy rescued from some barbed wire yesterday," her uncle explained. "But she was in a stall last night. How'd she get loose?"

This time both men shrugged. "We weren't in the barn till this morning," George said, "but I think there was an open stall door."

"I fastened it tight, Uncle Art," Wendy said. "I'm sure this time."

He nodded. "I think I know who our mysterious 'horse thief' was yesterday," he said. "I've known a lot of Shetland ponies with the talent, but not too many horses do it."

"What?" Wendy asked, puzzled.

"That silly filly is a gate opener. A real pro."

The two ranch hands moaned. "You want us to go after her?" George asked.

Uncle Art shook his head. "No use. She's half-wild. I don't think you could find her. We'll talk about it over breakfast. Did you finish the feeding already?"

Cliff shook his head. "We came right up to tell you about the filly."

"Okay, go ahead and feed the stock, then turn the cows out and saddle up our horses. Wendy can look around for the filly while we ride out to bring the dude horses in from the south pasture."

The men nodded. "Which horse shall I saddle for you, Wendy?" Cliff asked.

"I'll . . . look on foot," Wendy said, not meeting his eyes.

"The filly is very shy," Uncle Art said. "She may have more luck on foot."

"What's going on?" Aunt Laura asked, coming into the kitchen.

After hearing what had happened, Aunt Laura shook her head. "I hope the sheriff finds her owner soon. A horse like that can be a menace on a ranch."

"What do you do with a horse like Gypsy around?" Wendy asked her uncle.

He shrugged. "Tie the gates or lock them. That will keep her from opening them, but it's a bad habit on a ranch. If there were some sort of emergency and we needed the gates open in a hurry, we'd be in trouble."

97

Wendy swallowed hard, wishing that her uncle's words didn't bother her so. It wasn't her place to defend Gypsy, she reminded herself sternly. She had helped the filly when she needed help. But Wendy couldn't allow herself to become involved. Gypsy's owner would be coming to claim her. . . .

Wendy pushed her thoughts away and concentrated on helping her aunt prepare breakfast.

Cliff and George returned, washed up, and heaped their plates with sausages, eggs, and hashed brown potatoes. As they sat down, Cliff said, "About that filly, boss. . . ."

"What about her?" Uncle Art asked quickly.

"Well, she hit the door like a cannon. Near scared me to death. But soon as she was clear, she slowed up. She was limping—bad."

"Limping?" Wendy gasped.

"While we were feeding the stock, I remembered you mentioning wire. I figure she might have some infection." Cliff looked concerned.

Wendy started to get up, her breakfast untouched. "I'd better go look for her now," she said.

"You eat first," Aunt Laura insisted. "She may

not be so easy to find, and you'll need something warm inside to keep you going."

Wendy had trouble choking down the food, but somehow she managed it. Then she asked for permission to go after the filly.

Uncle Art nodded. "Look along the stream," he said. "And if you bring her in, tie the stall door shut so at least we'll know she'll stay where she is." He got up and looked at the two ranch hands. "You two about ready to go after the dude herd?" he asked.

Wendy started for the door.

"You'd better wear a jacket," her aunt called. "And take a rope and a small bucket of oats. If she's hungry enough, she'll find you."

When she came out of the barn with the rope and oat bucket, Wendy saw that the big corral was empty and the gates had been hooked open. In the south, near the boundary fence, she saw three riders. Sighing, Wendy set off, walking toward the highway, following the stream.

After nearly an hour of tramping around without seeing anything except the fat red and white Hereford cows, Wendy turned back. She hated giving up, but she realized that she wasn't going to find the filly by just walking around.

Maybe Gypsy was back at the barn, waiting, she thought hopefully. But as she neared the ranch buildings, Wendy knew Gypsy wouldn't be there. She heard the shouts of the men bringing in the horse herd. Running clumsily, she managed to reach the barn in time to watch the twenty-five horses streaming into the corral. She searched the herd eagerly. It was quickly obvious that Gypsy wasn't among the dude horses.

"Well, did you find the wayward sorrel?" Cliff asked, riding over.

Wendy shook her head. "You didn't see her, did you?" she asked.

"We saw some of her handiwork," George said, coming over with Uncle Art to join them. "The south pasture gate was open."

"Do you think she might be down there?" Wendy asked, her hopes rising.

"She has been," Cliff said, "but she may have wandered in that way. No one's been down to check that gate since early Friday."

"Maybe I should go down there and look for her," Wendy said.

"You can't go on foot," her uncle said quietly. "It's too far, and you'd get lost. Only a horse could find the way back home from there."

100

Wendy swallowed hard, trying to think of Gypsy instead of the nervous feeling his words started in her stomach. "Do you think she'll come back tonight, as she did last night?" she asked.

Her uncle shrugged. "Depends on how badly frightened she was this morning. All the activity around here today may keep her away. And, of course, a lot depends on how bad the infection is."

"She didn't look too good," Cliff contributed. "I don't think she'll get too far on a bad leg."

"Do you want us to look for her?" George asked. "She might be too sick to hide from us."

"She'd never let you find her," Wendy said, feeling terrible at the thought of Gypsy's suffering. "It'll have to be me, won't it, Uncle Art?"

Her uncle nodded, his eyes speculative. "Not on foot, though. We have a gentle old mare, Wendy. She's not so very fast, but Ladybug takes care of her riders. Would you like to give her a try?"

Wendy closed her eyes, fighting the rising sickness of fear, then nodded. "I have to find Gypsy," she said. "I'm the only one who can."

# 8 · Down and Out

THE HORSE her uncle led toward her was far
from a beauty, but she was friendly. Not that it
made any difference, Wendy thought, fear burn-
ing in her throat. It wasn't the horse that mattered; it was the sickness inside her—the way the
whole world seemed to twist under her feet
when she even thought about mounting.

"Why don't you fellows start by catching the
roughest dude stock?" Uncle Art suggested,
sensing that Wendy didn't want the two ranch
hands watching her. "They'll need the bucks
ridden out before our guests can use them."

Cliff and George turned away, taking the
ropes from their saddles and going into the corral with the milling horses. Uncle Art let Wendy
watch them for a moment, then asked, "Would
it help if I gave you a boost up onto her?"

Wendy shook her head, wondering if she was going to be sick or faint. "Where should I look for Gypsy?" she asked, hoping that her worry about the filly would give her the strength to mount.

"Well, if she has infection, it'll make her hot and thirsty, and she'll likely stay near the stream. Ride along it slowly and look for small hoof-prints. Her feet are a lot tinier than any of the dude horses, so they should be easy to pick out."

Wendy nodded, then clenched her teeth as she gathered the reins and slipped her left foot into the stirrup. She swayed for an instant, eyes closed, then swung her bad leg up and over and settled into the saddle. Her stomach tightened into a solid knot, and she winced.

"You okay?" her uncle asked.

Wendy nodded, her hands so icy she could hardly feel the reins as she tightened them and turned the mare away. "I'll be back as soon as I can," she said, swallowing her nausea and taking deep breaths of the cold, fresh morning air. *Gypsy,* she thought. *I have to find Gypsy. Nothing else matters.* Ladybug walked along calmly, unaware of the battle of nerves taking place on her back.

103

By the time they reached the gate to the south pasture, Wendy thought she'd won the first round. The knot in her stomach was still there, but she could look around, dismount, and open the gate, then force herself to mount again. Maybe her uncle was right, she told herself— perhaps, in time, she'd get over what had happened.

Clinging to that thought, Wendy guided the mare toward the stream and began watching the soft banks for small hoofprints. She'd ridden only a short distance before a high-pitched whinny reached her ears. Ladybug answered.

"Gypsy?" Wendy called. "Where are you, girl?"

Forgetting everything else, she kicked the mare into a rocking-chair lope, trusting her to follow the sound. Ladybug seemed to understand what was expected, and, in a few minutes, Wendy saw a flash of reddish hide in the brush ahead. She reined in and slid quickly from the saddle.

"Gypsy!" she called. "Where are you, girl? Are you all right?"

There was a flurry of movement ahead, then the filly limped into the open. Wendy's heart

dropped. Gypsy didn't look at all like the horse she'd seen through her window that first day at the ranch. One front leg was swollen, her head was down, and the small ears drooped pitifully. Wendy took only a few seconds to pet the filly and try to soothe her, knowing she must get help as soon as possible.

It was an unpleasant ride back, with the filly alternately fighting the rope and limping along so painfully that Wendy hated to keep her moving. Uncle Art was waiting to open the gate for her, his powerful stallion standing beside him. Gypsy saw Uncle Art and began feebly to fight the lead. But Wendy had tied the rope to her saddle horn, and Ladybug had enough quarter horse blood to work with the rope.

"Take her right to the barn and put her in her stall," Uncle Art said. "I'll tell Cliff and George to stay away from her, then I'll call the vet."

The seriousness of his tone told Wendy that she'd been right about the filly's condition. Talking to her comfortingly, she used the mare's strength to guide the protesting filly through the gate, then along the pasture toward the corral.

106

Gypsy followed more easily after Uncle Art galloped away on Happy.

As Wendy neared the corral, Cliff called, "Just leave Ladybug with the reins hanging; we'll get her after you're inside." Then he and George disappeared around the far side of the barn. Wendy rode right up to the corral, slid off the mare, and untied the rope. Gypsy seemed exhausted now. She stood with her head hanging and seemed scarcely to feel the pressure on the rope as Wendy urged her toward the barn.

Once in her stall, Gypsy paid no attention to the water or feedbox of oats that Wendy had left for her. Her body was radiating the heat of fever. When the barn door opened, she didn't even lift her head.

Uncle Art came in slowly. "Dr. James is on his way out," he said.

"What'll we do?" Wendy asked. "She acts as if she's awfully sick."

When Uncle Art opened the stall door, Gypsy tried to turn to face him. Her bad leg refused to hold her any longer, though, and she fell into the straw with a heavy thud. Uncle Art dropped beside her instantly, holding her head down to keep her from getting up. "Help me tie her hind legs, Wendy," he said. "Then she'll be ready for Doc when he gets here."

Later, Wendy sat at the filly's head, stroking her gently while Uncle Art and the veterinarian examined and worked over Gypsy. After a weak struggle, Gypsy resigned herself to their attentions and didn't move, even when the vet gave her several shots.

"What do you think, Doc?" Uncle Art asked when the vet finally gathered up his instruments and stepped out of the stall.

"She's a mighty sick horse," he said, "but I think we've caught the infection in time. I can't say for sure, of course. I'll come back tonight and give her another injection. We'll know more by then."

"Is there anything I can do for her?" Wendy asked.

The vet smiled. "Stay with her, keep her quiet, and, when the fever breaks, give her some mash —if she'll eat it." He looked around. "It might be a good idea to keep her covered, too. It's cold today, and they're forecasting snow for tonight."

"Snow?" Wendy looked at him in disbelief.

"A late storm blowing down from Canada,"

the veterinarian said. "It's a good thing you found her. With that leg, she'd never have lasted through a storm."

Uncle Art walked out with the vet, then came back with a heavy blanket. With Wendy's help, it was easily spread over the quiet filly. "We'll put the water down where she can reach it without getting up," he said. "Then it's time for us to have some food."

"Do you think she'll be all right?" Wendy asked. "I don't really want to leave her."

"She'll be fine," her uncle assured her. "We'll leave her legs tied for now so she can't get up. Then you can stay with her while we're out this afternoon."

"Out where?" Wendy asked.

"We'll have to round up the cows and calves. I can't leave them out in the snow. Some of the calves are far too young."

"But where will you put them?" Wendy asked, thinking of the dude horses in the big corral.

Uncle Art laughed. "It happens every spring. Happy will have to give up his paddock for a while. I'll put the dude horses in there, and he can stay in the barn with the mares and foals till after the storm." His face grew serious as

109

he studied the sky outside. "We'll have to hurry, too," he said. "That storm isn't far away."

"Will you need me?" Wendy asked. "I mean, to help round up the cattle?"

"I think we can manage," he said as he gave her shoulder a squeeze. "I know how hard it was for you to ride this morning. You did save the filly's life, though, so I think it was worth it."

The mention of her having ridden sent a surge of nausea through Wendy, but she forced it down and smiled weakly. "Gypsy is safe now," she said quietly.

Dinner was a hurried meal, with all eyes constantly turning toward the sky—which was fast turning from blue to gray as the heavy clouds rolled in from the northwest. "Leave the dishes," Aunt Laura said when they finished eating. "We can do them when we get back." Aunt Laura was wearing heavy woolen pants and a thick sweater, and when the five of them stepped outside, Wendy could understand why her aunt had insisted that she wear a sweater under her heavy jacket. The air was icy now.

Wendy watched apprehensively as her aunt and uncle rode off with Cliff and George, though she knew they were all accustomed to the changeable Montana climate. She felt deeply the responsibility of being alone with Gypsy.

She found the filly lying just as they'd left her. For a moment she was glad, but when Gypsy didn't even stir as she opened the stall door, all her fear flooded back. Her hand was shaking as she reached out to touch the filly. There was no response, though the filly's flesh radiated heat like a furnace.

"Oh, Gypsy," Wendy whispered. "Gypsy, please don't die."

One ear moved, and there was a weak flicker of life in the brown eye that was visible. Remembering a long-ago illness of her own, Wendy got up, brought a clean rag from the tack room, dipped it into the water, and began sponging the filly's hot, dry head. She pulled back the sides of the filly's mouth and squeezed some water inside.

An hour passed, then another. Wendy left Gypsy only to go to the door occasionally, watching for her aunt and uncle and the herd. The wind was shaking the buildings now, and the swirling snowflakes grew thicker and thicker.

Suddenly, dark shapes began drifting toward the corral. Wendy waited and held the barn door for her aunt as she came in leading the four horses. The men were feeding and bedding the cattle in the corral.

"How is she doing?" Aunt Laura asked, coming to stand by the stall, coated with snow and looking like a melting ghost.

"I'm worried about her," Wendy said. "She's so sick, Aunt Laura. I don't know what to do."

"It looks as if you've been doing all you can," her aunt said calmly.

"But she's not getting any better!" Wendy whimpered as she looked down at the filly's still form.

"Sometimes they don't," her aunt said quietly. "You have to face that, Wendy. She's a stray, and she may be weak from poor care. You've done all you can."

"She has to live—" Wendy began, then clamped her lips together. "Can you call the vet again? Maybe he could do something."

Aunt Laura sighed, and Wendy could see the weariness in her face. "He said he'd come tonight—if he can get through the storm. It's pretty bad out there right now."

"But—" Wendy began.

"I'm going up to the house to fix something

112

hot for all of us," Aunt Laura said. "Have Art look at her before you come up."

"I'm going to stay here," Wendy said.

"You have to eat."

"I can't leave her." Wendy knelt beside the filly once more.

Aunt Laura stood for another moment, then sighed and went out into the storm. Wendy sat alone beside Gypsy for what seemed like hours. Finally the door opened, and Uncle Art came in. "How is she?" he asked.

"I don't know," Wendy said.

"I'll look her over while you go and get some hot food," he said, pulling back the blanket to look at the filly's leg. "I'm going to try some compresses on that leg."

"I can help you," Wendy said, not wanting to leave even though her stomach was rumbling for food.

"You go eat some of Laura's chili and tell her I need a hot Epsom salts solution for a compress."

"Will that help?"

"Depends on how much good the shots did. If the antibiotic is working, and if I can bring the infection to a head, maybe we can whip it."

"Do you think the vet will come?"

113

"If he can make it, he'll be here. Now go and eat."

Reluctantly, Wendy turned away and limped to the barn door. Her leg ached from hours of kneeling. The storm took her breath away the moment she opened the door, and it was several seconds before she could make out the dim bulk of the house through the swirling snow. Hurrying as well as she could, Wendy headed for it.

The aroma of chili warmed and revived her as she entered the house. As soon as she had asked for the salts solution, she allowed the hot food and the warmth of the kitchen to absorb all her attention. It was nearly half an hour before her thoughts returned to the barn. "I've got to get back to Gypsy, Aunt Laura," she said.

Her aunt nodded. "Here's the Epsom salts," she said, handing her a plastic jug that steamed, "but you may not need it now."

"Why not?"

"I just saw a car down there."

"The vet?" Wendy felt a lift of hope.

"The storm's let up a little, so I expect it is Dr. James," her aunt said.

Wendy shrugged into her heavy jacket and let herself out into the steadily falling snow.

114

The wind had dropped, but she was still cold when she opened the barn door.

"Did you bring the Epsom salts?" Uncle Art called.

"Right here," Wendy answered, hurrying forward with the jug.

"Here, let me take it." A red-haired boy about her age straightened up from where he'd been kneeling between Dr. James and Uncle Art.

"How is she?" Wendy asked, dropping down at Gypsy's head.

"Tonight will tell the tale," Dr. James said. "The crisis is coming. The shots will fight the infection, and hot compresses will localize it, but mostly it'll be up to her. Some worse cases make it, and some easier cases die. A lot depends on the fight in the horse."

"What can I do?" Wendy asked.

"Someone will have to change the compresses —that's about it. I'll be out early in the morning to check. If the infection localizes so I can lance the leg, it'll be all right."

"As long as you're here, will you check Dotted Doll for me?" Uncle Art asked. "She's about due to foal, and she had some trouble last year, remember?"

Dr. James got up and brushed off his knees. "Sure thing, Art. Kirk can show Wendy how to handle the compresses."

As the men moved along the aisle to Dotted Doll's stall, Wendy became more aware of the boy beside her. He grinned at her. "I'm Kirk Donahue, Wendy," he said. "Doc's my uncle."

"Hi," Wendy said shyly.

"Is this your filly?" Kirk asked as he folded one of the rags from the pile and dipped it into the hot water.

"Yes," Wendy said, then bit her lip as she realized what she'd said. "I mean, no, She's a stray that wandered onto the ranch. But I've been taking care of her and—"

"She's really a beauty."

"I just hope she'll be all right," Wendy said, a little sigh escaping her.

"Wonder who owns her," Kirk said. "Working with my uncle, I've seen most of the horses in this part of the state, but I don't remember any like her."

Kirk chatted on as they worked over the filly, and Wendy found herself wanting to respond to the friendliness Kirk radiated. It was hard for her to keep from asking questions and returning

his implied offers of friendship, but Wendy reminded herself once more of the pain she'd be inviting—Kirk, like her Phoenix friends, would drop her like a hot potato if he ever heard about Buck. So she held herself aloof. She wasn't going to be hurt like that again.

She didn't think anyone but Kirk had noticed her reserve, but after he and the veterinarian had gone, Uncle Art said, "I know you're worried, Wendy, but I don't think that's any excuse for the cool way you treated Kirk. He's a nice boy, and he was trying to be friendly. You were hardly polite."

Wendy sighed. "I'm sorry," she said, knowing she couldn't explain why she preferred loneliness to the risk of a lost friendship.

"You'd better go on up to the house now."

Wendy shook her head. "I'm staying with Gypsy," she said.

"Nonsense. I can manage alone."

Wendy settled herself and gently lifted the filly's head into her lap so she could caress her. "Dr. James said she had to want to live. Maybe if she knows I love her, she will."

For a moment Uncle Art seemed ready to argue, but then he gave in. "Don't forget to

118

change the compress every time it cools. I'll bring you more hot water later."

"Thank you," Wendy said, not even looking up. Her whole concentration was on Gypsy, willing the filly to feel her love and to respond to it.

# 9 · Antisocial

THE HOURS became a blur. Wendy talked to Gypsy till her throat ached and her eyes burned from the strain of staying open. Gypsy's legs had long since been untied, but the filly made no attempt to move.

To keep awake, Wendy moved around within the narrow confines of the stall. In the weak light from her flashlight, she found marks on the filly's side—welts that looked suspiciously like the marks from a whip.

"How could anyone hurt you, Gypsy?" Wendy asked, following the marks with the light. "Why would anyone do it?"

"Do what?"

Wendy jumped up and turned. It was Aunt Laura. "I didn't hear you come in," Wendy said.

"You look half-dead."

"I'm fine." Wendy straightened. "I was just looking Gypsy over. She's got welts on her side. I think she's been whipped."

"Are you sure?" Aunt Laura knelt to examine the filly. "She has been hurt, that's for certain. I'm not positive she was whipped, but that could explain why she's so afraid of men."

"If her owner did that, you won't send her back to him, will you?" Wendy asked.

"We haven't even found him yet," her aunt said, not answering her question.

"But you can't . . . I mean—" Wendy found her face wet with sudden tears. "She's been hurt enough! Maybe she ran away because her owner mistreated her. She might even die because of what he did to her. He doesn't deserve to have her back."

Aunt Laura put a comforting arm around Wendy's shoulders. "We won't let your Gypsy go back until we're sure she won't be hurt. I promise."

Wendy relaxed, believing the words because she wanted to. "She needs me to take care of her," she whispered, not adding the rest of what she felt—not admitting that she needed to love as desperately as Gypsy needed to be loved.

121

There was a stirring behind her, and Wendy felt her aunt's arm loosen. "You've done it, Wendy," Aunt Laura whispered. "Look!"

Wendy lifted her head, then laughed through the tears that had washed down her face. Gypsy had rolled over and was sitting up, looking like a big, clumsy dog, a confused expression in her mismatched eyes. As they watched, the filly tried to get up but was too weak to make it.

"Here, let's help her up," Aunt Laura said. "Then I'll make her a bucket of oat mash, and you can pin that blanket so it'll stay on her."

"You think she's all right?" Wendy asked as she and her aunt boosted the filly up onto all four legs.

"Feel her skin."

"She's cool!"

"Her fever's broken. She'll get well now." Aunt Laura examined the leg, which was much less swollen. "In fact, she'll probably heal as fast as she got sick. The antibiotics seem to have the infection stopped. The wound is clean, and the compresses have reduced the swelling. I'll bind a light dressing over her leg, and then we can go to bed."

Wendy protested about leaving the filly, but

her aunt was firm. "You've got tests tomorrow," she reminded her. "You have to get some sleep."

"I'm not tired now," Wendy said honestly as she used three oversize safety pins to secure the blanket around the filly. "I could stay here all night."

"From the way she's eating that mash, I really don't think there's any need," Aunt Laura said. "Now, you get on up to the house, while I check on Dotted Doll."

Wendy hesitated only long enough to stroke the filly's neck, then tied the stall door shut and headed for the barn door, her weariness returning as her excitement faded. She scarcely noticed the still air outside, not even realizing that the storm was over.

In her room, Wendy undressed quickly, then stopped to inspect the kittens before getting into bed. They were getting livelier and crawling about inside the suitcase, but their eyes were still tightly closed. They were beginning to develop differences, too. One had a white throat and white paws, another showed several shades of brown mixed with the black, and the third was pure black.

"I hope you plan to stay indoors till morning,

Abigail," Wendy said as she stood at the window looking out over the fascinating expanse of white land. Even the trees seemed dressed up, with every limb gracefully ruffled. It was a beautiful but alien sight after her years of desert living. "It's too cold to leave the window open. We'd all freeze."

The calico cat went on washing her black kitten, without looking up. Wendy drew the drapes, hoping that they'd help to keep out some of the cold. Being in bed felt good to her sore and aching muscles. It had been a very long day.

Wendy was not the first one up the next morning. She awoke to the sounds of voices and the smells of breakfast. She pulled on her clothes in a hurry, anxious to go to the barn to see Gypsy, but when she came into the kitchen, Aunt Laura was filling the breakfast plates.

"Looks like you worked a miracle," Cliff said with a smile. "Your filly is ready to fight this morning."

"Really?" Wendy asked, anxious for word of Gypsy's condition.

"When I leaned over the stall door this morning, I got a good look at her hind feet," George

124

said, grinning. "She's just plain antisocial."

"She's been hurt," Wendy said. "I found welts on her side."

"We'll take our time with her," Uncle Art said. "She's a bright little thing, so it shouldn't take long to convince her that we want to be friends."

After breakfast, Uncle Art went with Wendy to inspect the filly. After a few moments of coaxing, Gypsy accepted molasses pellets from his hand.

"Silly filly," Uncle Art said. "Looks fine to me, but we'd better keep her inside till Doc comes out to give her another shot. Don't forget to tie her stall door, Wendy, or she'll have herself and all the rest of the horses out in no time."

Wendy spent most of the morning with Gypsy, grooming and petting her and talking to her. Uncle Art, Cliff, and George were in and out as they moved the horses back into their usual corrals and turned the cattle out to graze.

"Aren't you afraid we'll get another storm?" Wendy asked her uncle on one of his visits. "I mean, now that you've turned the cattle out again?"

"Oh, I'm *sure* we'll get another storm," he said, "and probably a worse one. I wouldn't have brought the cattle in if I'd known how little snow we'd get this time."

"Then why turn them out now?" Wendy asked.

"That's the ranching business, Wendy. I can't afford to feed them when they could be out grazing. We feed all during the winter, and my hay's about gone. The grazing is fine now, and this little snow will just green everything up nicely. As soon as the calves are a week or so older, we'll drive the whole herd south into the pasture where I had the dude horses. They'll be able to handle a late spring storm there without too much trouble."

"Then we'll just have the horses in?" Wendy asked.

"Only the ones we're working," he said. "Once we've ridden all the dude horses a few times, I'll put them in the lake meadow—the Appaloosa mares and foals, too, as soon as they're strong enough. I don't keep horses in when I'm not working them. I don't think standing around a corral all day is good for them."

"What horses will you keep in?" Wendy went on brushing Gypsy as they talked.

"The Appaloosas I'm breaking and training

126

and the yearlings. They're at an age where they need to be handled a lot—keeps them from getting too wild. Happy stays in, of course, and whatever horse you decide you want to ride."

Wendy sighed. "What about Gypsy?" she asked.

"By then she may have gone back to where she came from, Wendy," he warned. "We're bound to find her owner sooner or later."

Wendy busied herself with Gypsy's tangled mane, refusing even to look at her uncle.

At noon, when Wendy saw her aunt dressed up, she remembered that today was the day she was supposed to take her school tests.

"I pressed your jumper for you," Aunt Laura said. "You can change after lunch, then we'll go in and do some shopping."

Wendy nodded, though she longed to forget everything else and just spend the rest of the day with Gypsy. She dreaded even going near a school.

Littleville was small, and the stores lacked the vast displays she was used to, but all the clerks were friendly, and everyone seemed anxious to welcome her to town. By the time four o'clock neared, Wendy and her aunt could hardly carry all the packages of patterns, materials, notions, and yarn to the car.

"We've got materials for a whole year's sewing and knitting," her aunt said gaily. "You'll be busy till this time next year trying to get everything done!"

"I went overboard," Wendy admitted, "but I can hardly wait to start. I wish we could go straight home now and start on everything."

"Wait'll your uncle sees all of this," Aunt Laura said with a grin. "But then, he's used to my shopping sprees."

They were still giggling like sisters when her aunt parked in front of the combination junior high and high school building. "Here you are," Aunt Laura said, then, sensing Wendy's apprehension, added, "I'll go in with you and help you find Peg's room. I'm afraid most everybody's gone by now; classes were out about half an hour ago."

"I hope the tests won't take too long," Wendy said. "It'll make you awfully late getting home to fix dinner."

"I'll do some grocery shopping while you're racking your brains," Aunt Laura said. "Dinner is no problem; I left a casserole. We'll eat—if Art remembers to turn on the oven, of course."

The school was quiet, and the halls were empty, but it still brought back ugly memories. When they reached the empty classroom, it took all of Wendy's strength just to say good-bye to Aunt Laura and sit down at a desk.

Once alone, Wendy felt the familiar panic closing in on her. She tried to fight it, reminding herself that there were no classes coming—no faces full of questions—just a teacher and a few tests. She'd be able to study alone in her room on the ranch. Nobody would ask her about Buck.

Suddenly she was back in the Phoenix apartment, dressing slowly while her father called to her to hurry. He was waiting to drive her to school that morning, her first day back in class since the accident.

Her father had talked cheerfully about how good it would feel to get back to school and see all her friends again . . . that he was sure she wouldn't have any trouble making up the work she'd missed. He hadn't mentioned Buck since the accident, and Wendy had decided not to tell him about her trip to the stable and learning of Buck's death.

129

More than anything else, Wendy dreaded going back to school. How could she face her friends? And how could she face Gretchen? Everyone who knew Wendy knew about her dream of having Buck for her very own, and now everybody surely knew that she had killed him. What would they say? What would they be thinking?

"I can't go in," Wendy said when her father parked in front of the school. "It's too soon."

"Nonsense," he said good-naturedly. "It's been weeks. I should think you'd be bored with sitting around by yourself all the time. Haven't you missed your friends?"

Yes! Yes, she'd missed them—especially Gretchen. Gretchen had not come to visit at the hospital. She hadn't called or even sent a card. And now Wendy couldn't face her. She couldn't face any of them.

Wendy slid out of the car, not giving her father a chance to question her. The final buzzer was ringing as she limped down the nearly empty corridor and into her classroom, not daring to look around. She waited till she was seated at her desk before lifting her head.

Everyone was staring at her. Everyone was

130

turned around, looking—everyone but Gretchen, her best friend. Gretchen, who had shared her love of riding and horses, who had encouraged her to take riding lessons, whose father had owned Buck—Gretchen was facing forward.

Wendy heard the rumble of her teacher's voice but not the words. The sickness rose in her throat, and she knew she couldn't stay. She couldn't face the accusations, the questions, that would come when the class was over.

Not really aware of what she was doing, Wendy rose and made her way out of the classroom. The rest was a blur—being taken to the principal's office by her teacher . . . waiting for her father . . . refusing to answer his questions on the endless drive home—

"Hi, Wendy! Ready for the brain strain?" A friendly voice rescued her from the quicksand of her memories. It was Kirk Donahue.

"Oh, hi," she gulped, embarrassed by the way she was shaking. "I didn't hear you come in."

"You looked like you were a million miles away. Is it your filly?" His genuine concern broke through the coolness Wendy was trying to hide behind.

"No, she's much better." Wendy described the

events of the night before, using them to drive back her horrible memories. Finally she asked, "What are you doing here?"

Kirk scowled. "Making up a test I missed last week. That's why Mrs. Carter is late. She's thinking up some extra-hard questions for me." He grinned. "I've been talking to your aunt—inviting you to the Saddle Club meeting."

"The what?"

"It's a town thing. Everybody belongs. We go on rides and hold gymkhanas in the summer, and in the winter we have parties and dances. The meeting is a week from tomorrow. We'll be planning the first big ride of the season. It'll give you a chance to meet just about everybody in town."

"I don't think—" Wendy began, but the door opened, interrupting her, and Mrs. Carter came in with a sheaf of papers.

Before they had time to discuss the Saddle Club further, Wendy and Kirk were too deep in tests to think of anything else. And by the time Wendy finished her last one, Kirk was already long gone.

"How was it?" Mrs. Carter asked when Wendy turned in the papers.

"Not too bad," Wendy said. "Most of it I had earlier this year, and I could remember quite a bit. Toward the end there were things I didn't know, though. I hope I did all right."

"I'm sure you did." Mrs. Carter smiled. "I just have to know where you stand in comparison to the rest of my seventh graders. You take these textbooks with you and run along now; I'm sure Laura's waiting for you. When I get the tests checked, I'll call you and give you a few assignments. Then you can come in for some tutoring next Tuesday."

"Thank you, Mrs. Carter," Wendy said. "See you then."

"Don't wait so long," Mrs. Carter called. "Why don't you ride over some afternoon? I know Carol would love to show you around our place."

The mention of riding sent a familiar shudder through Wendy's small frame. Things hadn't changed just because she had ridden out to find Gypsy, and Wendy knew it. If anything, she was more than ever convinced that riding was not for her. Why should she do something that made her sick? Why did everyone here consider riding and friendship a natural combination?

Wendy walked out to the car slowly, thinking

134

about the invitations from Kirk and Mrs. Carter. On the way home, her aunt was full of information about the Saddle Club and Wendy's future as a member.

Wendy was too tired to argue, but, deep inside, she was certain that she would not ride anymore—ever.

## 10 · Gypsy's Message

THE NEXT WEEK flew by on wings. With sewing, knitting, working on her school assignments, and playing and working with Gypsy, Wendy had no time to feel lonesome. After the snow, the weather had warmed once more, and Wendy spent her afternoons walking around the ranch, with Gypsy following her like a puppy.

No one mentioned riding, except once, when Uncle Art said, "I've got to turn the dude horses out tomorrow, Wendy. Have you decided which one you want me to keep in for you to ride?"

"Ladybug, I guess," Wendy said, not looking up from her knitting.

"Oh, honey, can't you pick one of the younger horses?" Aunt Laura asked. "Poor old Ladybug just couldn't take the long Saddle Club rides."

"Neither can I, Aunt Laura," Wendy blurted,

jumping up. "I think I'll go and see if Abigail needs food." She fled before they could question her further.

Watching the little fuzzy balls of fur rolling around in her suitcase, Wendy managed to push away thoughts of future Saddle Club rides, but she couldn't escape one fact: The Saddle Club meeting was tomorrow night. Kirk and Carol and all the young people her age would be there, and, though she longed to get acquainted, she dreaded it. Being alone on the ranch was relatively uncomplicated, but she sensed that once she started meeting more people, things would change.

"Could I take some sandwiches and go on a long hike tomorrow?" she asked when she rejoined her aunt and uncle in the living room.

"Where are you going?" Aunt Laura asked.

"I thought I'd go down to the lake. I like to sit there and watch the water."

"Why don't you ride?" Uncle Art asked. "You could go there and back in less than an hour."

"Gypsy and I would rather walk," Wendy said. "Besides, it's better for my leg. I hardly limp now, and my legs are almost the same size again." Wendy pulled up her jeans and stuck her feet out in front of her. Since she wore pants most of the time, the scars of her accident hadn't bothered her. She knew a time would come when she'd have to wear dresses, and she wanted her leg well by then.

"You aren't thinking of swimming, are you?" Aunt Laura asked with a mischievous grin.

"In that water? If it's like the stream, I'd freeze to death." Wendy shivered at the idea.

"Well, just don't try. It's too early in the year, and besides, no one should swim alone."

"I know that," Wendy said. "I just like to look at the lake. Guess it comes from living in the desert all this time."

"Didn't you have lakes around Phoenix?" Uncle Art asked.

"Not within hiking distance," Wendy said with a grin. "Is it all right, then?"

"I suppose so, as long as you're back early enough to take a bath and get cleaned up for the Saddle Club meeting. You are going to wear your new pantsuit, aren't you?"

Wendy nodded reluctantly. The rust-colored corduroy pantsuit was the product of several nights in the sewing room, and she *was* anxious to wear it—but not to the Saddle Club meeting.

Wednesday dawned bright and clear, and Wendy packed a large lunch, not forgetting to take a small bag of oats for Gypsy. They set off across the small home pasture, the meadowland that stretched between the corrals and the south fence. Once through the gate, Wendy took her time, following the stream for a while, seeking a place narrow enough to jump.

In her ramblings, she'd grown confident about finding her way back, though there were still two sections of the ranch she hadn't explored—the northwest and the southwest corners. Both areas were fenced off because of their roughness and the danger to horses and cattle.

There were trails, though, Uncle Art had told her, and even an unused back road that passed through part of the southwestern area. Wendy had avoided exploring there because the lake cliffs were too steep for easy climbing, and she hesitated to strain her weak leg.

Gypsy ranged far and wide, pausing to graze sometimes, then racing off at top speed, bucking and jumping with the sheer joy of being alive. But she always returned to sniff at Wendy's arm or to rest her head on Wendy's shoulder for a while before bounding away again.

139

Today Wendy angled toward the south. The best lake beach was just at the foot of the lake cliffs. There, the water had worn an inlet that was sheltered from the wind and had a smooth pebble beach.

Wendy was almost to the lake before she missed Gypsy. The filly had been with her when she left the meadow, but somewhere in the woods she had wandered off. Wendy whistled her three-note call she'd begun using to signal the filly, but there was no answering whinny or rattle of hooves. Not too upset, Wendy kept walking. She reached the beach alone.

She spread the small blanket on the smoothest stretch of sand and set the lunch sack on it, then took off her shoes and socks to wade a little in the icy lake water. There were boats racing around farther out from the shore, and Wendy watched them for a while, but her thoughts were on Gypsy, and she turned to check the woods constantly, hoping for a glimpse of bright sorrel hide. Several times she whistled, but there was still no reply.

An hour passed, and hunger began gnawing. Wendy, feeling very much abandoned, settled herself on the blanket and opened the lunch bag.

She ate the two sandwiches and piece of cake slowly, still hoping that Gypsy would come and share the apples she'd brought. Finally, however, she could stand it no longer. Folding up her blanket, Wendy started back the way she'd come, pausing every few minutes to whistle for the filly.

She was halfway home again before she first heard a whinny. It seemed to be coming from the south, and it sounded so sad that Wendy knew it couldn't be an answer to her whistle. Though she was getting tired, she turned south to investigate.

The ground grew rougher as she neared the rocky cliffs that separated the south pasture from the lakeshore. The whinnies were louder, and even though she still couldn't see Gypsy, Wendy was sure it was the filly. Fearing that she might be trapped somewhere and unable to come, Wendy ran through the last band of woods, then stopped as the brush gave way to an open stretch.

Gypsy was there, all right, but she wasn't paying any attention to Wendy's calls. Instead, the filly was leaning on the barbed wire fence, her nose into the wind. As Wendy watched, the small

141

horse began pacing up and down, pausing to whinny every few steps. The little ears were trained to the wind, listening for an answer.

Curious, Wendy crossed the rough ground to where the filly stood. "What is it, girl?" she asked, reaching out.

Gypsy whirled and raced away, then stopped about twenty yards from her, ears flipping forward and back, eyes white-ringed once more.

"What's the matter, Gypsy?" Wendy asked. "Don't you remember me? Did something frighten you? What happened?"

Slowly the tension seemed to drain from the filly's slender body, and after a few seconds, Gypsy came to her and accepted the oats. When they were gone, the filly followed Wendy back into the trees just as she had before. Still, Wendy couldn't forget the way she'd looked, nor could she understand the urgency of the filly's pacing and calling. Had she come from that direction? Wendy asked herself. Were the secrets of her past beyond that fence?

With that thought still troubling her at dinner, Wendy asked her aunt, "Who lives south of us, beyond the lake cliffs?"

"The next ranch is the Carters', but there's a

wide stretch of public land in between. It's sort of barren—too rocky for stock, so no one's ever done much with it. Why?"

"No reason," Wendy said, afraid to have anyone investigate, for fear they might find a clue that would send Gypsy back to her owner. "I was just down that way today and got to wondering."

"If you ever want to ride over to the Carters'," Uncle Art said, "it isn't too far by way of the lake. You have to ride in the shallow water around that first big cliff, but after that you can follow the beach. The Carter house is built on the lake side of their property, instead of close to the road, like ours."

"Maybe I will sometime," Wendy said, veering away from the subject of riding. She was already planning to walk along the cliff's top on her next hike. From there she should be able to see what Gypsy had found so interesting.

"I put Gypsy in with the other yearlings," Uncle Art said later when he came in from his nightly check of the horses. "I think she's bored with being in the barn. The corral has the kind of latch she shouldn't be able to reach from the inside."

Wendy nodded. "She probably won't want out

143

anyway, now that she's with other horses."

"She'll be fine while you're gone," Uncle Art assured her.

The Saddle Club meeting turned out to be both better and worse than she'd imagined. Kirk met her at the door and began introducing her to the other young members. She had no trouble making conversation, since Kirk or Carol had already mentioned Gypsy, and everyone seemed interested in the strange filly that had appeared out of nowhere.

Still, as they talked, Wendy couldn't help thinking of Gretchen and the times they'd talked of horses this way. Would all these young people turn away from her as Gretchen had? she asked herself. They were so friendly now—they knew she'd saved a horse's life. But what if they also knew that she'd killed Buck?

An old ache rose in her throat, ending her conversation. Wendy excused herself, waving an empty punch cup. Once in the kitchen, she leaned against the sink and stared out through the window at the darkness beyond, wishing that there were some way she could avoid being here and learning about all the fun she'd have to miss because she couldn't ride.

No close friends and no special horse—that had been her resolve before she came. Gypsy had broken that resolve once, and Wendy was sure it would end painfully. Better the loneliness of the ranch than the agony of losing another friend. She couldn't ride—couldn't be a part of the life here—so why should she try?

Suddenly Wendy's mind was snapped back to the present by one word in a conversation on the other side of the kitchen.

". . . Morgan. I told him there just weren't many of the breed in the area, but he said to keep an eye out. Seems the mare was extremely valuable and due to foal any day, which makes it more of a worry."

Wendy recognized the voice of the man speaking, one of the Saddle Club officers.

"What made him think the thieves would be coming this way?" the other man asked. "I'd think there'd be a better market in Colorado or California."

"Didn't say," the first man replied. "Just asked me to inquire around for a stray brown Morgan mare, probably with a foal at heel by this time."

"Well, I'll keep an eye open out our way, but I don't expect to. . . ." The man moved away, but

145

Wendy didn't follow. She had no desire to hear any more of the conversation.

A stolen Morgan mare didn't mean anything, she told herself. Gypsy might not even be a Morgan. Besides, they'd said nothing about a filly with one brown eye and one blue eye, and that was much more distinctive than a brown mare. Wendy tried to push the whole thing out of her mind, to pretend that she hadn't heard it at all. But for the rest of the evening, she cringed a little each time the man began to talk, fearful of what he might say.

It was a relief to climb into the station wagon with her aunt and uncle, and Wendy could hardly keep her eyes open on the drive back to the ranch. Aunt Laura and Uncle Art were busy discussing the upcoming ride, and Wendy could hear her name included in the plans, but she was too drowsy to object. She was nearly asleep when her uncle suddenly slammed on the brakes, careening the station wagon to a screeching halt.

"What was that?" Aunt Laura gasped.

"A horse," her uncle said, anger in his tone. "One of my yearlings."

"What's it doing out here on the road?" Aunt Laura asked.

"What happened?" Wendy looked around fearfully. "You didn't hit it, did you?"

"No, I didn't hit it, but it's no thanks to that blasted filly!"

"Gypsy?" Wendy had a sinking feeling. "I thought you said she couldn't work that kind of latch."

"Obviously I was wrong! She's turned the stock loose again. She's a menace, Wendy. I don't know what we're going to do with her."

Wendy said nothing, but a cold feeling started in the pit of her stomach and spread slowly through her. She had no doubt that her uncle would be delighted to hear the news about the missing Morgan mare. "I'll help you round them up in the morning," she said. "I'm sorry."

"That's not the point, Wendy. We'll have to do something about her before the guests start to arrive. I'm always careful on this road, but the guests can't be expected to watch for horses —one of the guests or one of the horses could be badly hurt in an accident if Gypsy keeps opening the gates. Maybe whoever owned that silly filly is glad to be rid of her!"

147

## 11 · Ladybug, Ladybug

THE TELEPHONE'S RINGING woke Wendy early the next morning. She rolled over to go back to sleep, but her aunt called, "Wendy—it's your father! Long distance!" She scrambled out of bed and into her robe.

Her father's voice sounded crackly and far-away but typically cheerful. "Hello, sweetheart! What are you doing in bed in the middle of the afternoon? It's teatime!"

They chatted happily, after her father assured Wendy that his company was paying the phone bill. Wendy had so many things to tell him, it seemed as though she had been on the ranch all summer. Most of her conversation was about Gypsy, though.

"Daddy," Wendy blurted after telling him about Gypsy's illness, "will you . . . help me buy her? When we find her owner, I mean? She'll never be happy with anyone else but me, and—"

"Wait a minute, now," he interrupted. "In your letters you've said that you still aren't riding."

"Yes, Daddy, but—"

"Well, a horse is a little large for a pet if you're not going to ride. What would you do with her when she got full-grown—walk her like a dog?" There was gentle humor in his voice, but his words stung.

"But her owner—" Wendy moaned. "What if he mistreats her? There were welts on her side!"

"That's between the horse and its owner, Wendy; you know that. You can't go around buying every animal that's mistreated by its owner. Now, if you were riding—"

"Oh, Daddy, I've tried! Really I have! Gypsy *needs* me!"

"Well. . . ." His conviction wavered. "Your uncle is the best judge of horses I know. I'll leave it up to him. He has a special bank account for your expenses, though I'm sure he never—"

"Oh, thank you, Daddy! You're wonderful!"

"Don't thank me—talk to your uncle. If I know him, he'll take more convincing than I did!"

149

Wendy gulped, realizing that he was right.

They both said good-byes, assuring one another that they were doing fine and would continue to write. Even though she missed her father, Wendy felt wonderful when she hung up the phone. She only wished he could be here to see Gypsy for himself. He'd understand, Wendy was sure.

When she went into the kitchen for breakfast, Cliff and George were just coming in from feeding the stock.

"Hey, Wendy, that filly of yours is missing again," Cliff said, his tone telling her that he wasn't too concerned.

"I know," Wendy said with a sigh. "She let the yearlings loose last night. I'm going to help Uncle Art round them up after breakfast."

"No need," George said. "They were all standing around waiting for breakfast this morning. All we had to do was shut the gate."

Wendy started to laugh with relief, then realized what Cliff had said first. "You mean Gypsy wasn't with them?" she asked.

George shook his head. "I thought maybe you'd put her in the barn, but she's nowhere around."

150

"Who's missing?" Uncle Art asked, coming into the kitchen.

"Gypsy didn't come back with the other young horses," Wendy said. "I think I'd better go look for her, don't you?"

"I suppose so," her uncle said, "but I suspect she'll come wandering back when she gets hungry for oats. I had planned on having you here to help me halterbreak the foals."

"Today?" Wendy was surprised. "They're still so little."

"I want to turn them out in the lake pasture tomorrow, so they have to be ready. They don't learn too much in the first lessons, anyway, but I've found that by doing it this early, they're easier to handle in the fall." He sipped his coffee. "What did your father have to say?"

"I asked him about buying Gypsy," Wendy confessed, knowing this was not the best time to discuss it.

"What did he say?"

"That he'd leave it up to you, because you know about horses."

"I'm not sure I know about that one," her uncle said, shaking his head. "She's nothing but trouble."

151

"She's just been hurt, that's all," Wendy said. "You can't blame her for being afraid if she's been abused. And you can't send her back to someone who'd beat her."

"Hey, now, take it easy. I'm not going to let the little monster be abused. I just think you're getting a little ahead of yourself. We haven't found her owner yet, and we don't know that he's the one who put those marks on her. She could be a chronic wanderer, and if she is, there's no telling where she's been."

Wendy opened her mouth to argue, then closed it. Though she longed to have Gypsy's future settled, she sensed that this was the wrong time to force the issue.

"I'll go look for Gypsy right after breakfast," she said, her mind already picturing the filly pacing up and down by the fence that separated the lake pasture and the cliff area. She felt sure that she'd find Gypsy there again. All she'd have to do, she thought wryly, was follow the trail of open gates. At least that way she'd know which pasture Gypsy was in.

Riding was not such a simple matter, though. Wendy tried not to think about it while she dressed and Cliff saddled Ladybug for her. But

152

when she saw the horse, saddled and waiting, Wendy's stomach began to churn. Cliff had gone back to the house; there was nobody else around.

Wendy staggered out behind the barn and was sick. She waited there for several minutes, wishing she could go back to the house and go to bed—at the same time, hoping no one would see her and make her do just that. She had to find Gypsy.

Finally, after a drink of icy water from the pump, Wendy went back into the barn, closed her eyes, and climbed up into the saddle.

It didn't take long to discover that she'd been wrong about the filly heading for the lake pasture. That gate was still latched. Still feeling uncomfortable in the saddle but driven by worry, Wendy turned the gentle Ladybug south, letting her lope across the thick grass of the home pasture. Sure enough, the next gate was open.

Wendy rode through, closing the gate behind her, then stopped to think. Had she been wrong about the filly's interest in the cliff area? she asked herself. Or was Gypsy coming this way because she'd discovered there was no gate between the lake pasture and the cliffs? There was only one way to find out.

Wendy headed for the fence line and rode along it, trying to remember if her uncle had mentioned a gate in this section. She was almost sure he had, saying something about a back road that ran through the area beyond. The land on the other side of the fence was rough and offered little grazing. Wendy couldn't help wondering why Gypsy would want to go into such a bleak part of the ranch.

In her hurry to find the filly, Wendy kept Ladybug moving along at her slow lope, not allowing the old mare her usual pauses for bites of grass and slowing her only to send the three-note whistle. After the third call, Ladybug lifted her head and pricked up her ears, as though she'd heard something or perhaps caught a scent on the breeze. Eager, Wendy urged her to move faster.

They came over the rise at a good clip, and Wendy could see the open gate ahead. She had no time to see anything more. Ladybug stumbled and went to her knees, pitching Wendy out of the saddle, over her head, and onto the hard, rocky ground.

Wendy lay still for several seconds, waiting for the darkness to clear. Very carefully, she got

154

up. She ached in a dozen places, but nothing seemed broken. Immediately her thoughts went to Ladybug. The mare was standing a few feet away, calmly cropping the sparse grass.

"Are you all right, old girl?" Wendy asked, feeling guilty as she examined the small cuts on the heavy knees. She'd had no business loping her for so long without a rest. Just because poor Ladybug was good and obedient didn't give Wendy the right to tire the old horse out.

A whinny from the other direction turned her head, and Wendy looked up to see Gypsy standing atop the cliffs, looking like a painting against the background of deep blue sky. An echoing whinny drifted up from the canyons, but Wendy didn't hear it. She was whistling for the filly.

Gypsy danced along the hard, rocky cliff, then bounded out of sight along what must have been the old road. Wendy whistled again, then picked up the reins to lead Ladybug out of the brush so she could mount.

Her heart dropped as the old mare limped forward. Wendy bent down to give Ladybug's knees a closer inspection. She wouldn't be riding the old mare anymore today. Nothing was broken, but the mare's right leg was strained

156

and swelling—riding would only make it worse.

"I'm sorry, girl," Wendy said. *Careless, stupid, not fit to ride a horse* . . . the old accusations filled her mind, and Wendy couldn't argue. "Never again!" she told herself. Then, leaving the reins trailing, she took the lead rope from her saddle and started down the hill on foot.

Gypsy reappeared before she reached the gate. "Come on, girl," Wendy called. "We've got to get back to the ranch, and it's going to be a long walk."

Gypsy came close and then danced away, obviously wanting Wendy to chase her. But Wendy was too shaken by what had happened to Ladybug. "Come on," she said firmly. "Stop being such a monster, or I'll never be able to keep you."

Startled by the stern tone, Gypsy allowed Wendy to tie the lead rope to her halter, then came through the gate obediently. Wendy latched the gate, wishing that she'd remembered to bring an extra piece of rope to tie it shut. She didn't like the filly going into the rugged area. There were too many places for her to get into trouble.

It was a long, slow journey back to the ranch,

and the sun was nearly overhead by the time Wendy led the two horses across the home pasture. Uncle Art had been watching for her, and he was there to take Ladybug's reins even before she reached the barn. "What happened?" he asked, studying the horse's slightly swollen knee.

"She stumbled and went down on some rocks." Wendy winced as she felt fresh pangs of guilt. "We were loping, and I guess I wasn't watching where we were going. Is it serious?"

"Watching doesn't always help with a horse as old as Ladybug," Uncle Art said. "She's just not quick enough to recover her balance anymore. It doesn't look bad, though. You won't be able to ride her for a while. I'll keep her in for a day or two, then turn her out with the others. You'll just have to pick another riding horse."

"No, thanks," Wendy said. "I'm not riding anymore."

"You shouldn't feel that way," Uncle Art said. "There's no real damage done. A few days' rest will cure the bruise, and a week or two in the pasture will have her fit again." He turned his attention to Gypsy. "Where did you find this troublemaker?" he asked.

"Out by the cliffs. She seems to like that area."

158

Wendy put Gypsy in her stall and tied it shut firmly.

"She may have come in that way," her uncle mused. "It's about the only section of the ranch that has a gate to the outside. Everything else is securely fenced." He carried Wendy's saddle to the tack room, then said, "Let's go and eat. You're going to need more strength than you think for those foals."

Her uncle was right about her needing all her muscles. The little foals, so docile when they were following their mothers, proved to be stronger than she'd expected and quite willing to fight. Her arms felt as though they'd been dragged out of their sockets by the time she freed the last little colt to go bucking back to his mother.

"You handle horses very well," her uncle said. "I noticed it with Gypsy, of course, but you're just as good with these little fellows."

"I always used to dream of owning and training horses," Wendy said simply. "I think I read every book the library had on that subject."

"There's no reason why you can't own and raise horses here," her uncle said. "I've got three two-year-olds just waiting for someone to work them, not to mention five yearlings that are ready to start."

"I'd love to work with them," Wendy said, "but when it comes time to ride—"

"I've watched you, Wendy. You could handle any of the horses on this ranch without any trouble. You have good instincts. You think of your horse first—like leading Ladybug home so you wouldn't strain her leg, or rescuing that crazy filly from the wire by using a blindfold. Your feeling for horses shows in your riding ability. You can't let a couple of accidents keep you from using a real talent."

Wendy kicked at the dirt. "I've got a talent, all right," she said bitterly. "Every time I ride a horse, it gets hurt—or killed. I wasn't watching when Buck hit the pickup, just like I wasn't watching today when Ladybug fell. I'm *dangerous* to a horse—any horse—when it comes to riding."

"I'll let you ride Happy anytime you want to," Uncle Art said. "You know I trust you with him. He's my pride and joy, but I know you'd treat him right."

Wendy just shook her head. "I can't risk another horse's life, Uncle Art. Maybe I'm just

160

bad luck. If another one got hurt . . . well, I'd never forgive myself."

Her uncle sighed. "You shouldn't give up like that, Wendy. You just have to forget the past. I promise you, everything will be all right."

"Maybe, someday," she said. "But I'm not ready yet. I'll do the groundwork for you, but no more riding—okay?"

He shrugged, offering no more argument, for which Wendy was grateful. She realized that he'd meant everything he said, even the offer of letting her ride the beautifully trained stallion. But she couldn't match his confidence with her own courage.

"Are you going to turn the mares out now?" she asked to change the subject.

"I'll take them out tomorrow, and Ladybug, too, if her leg doesn't swell anymore."

"What if we get another storm?" Wendy asked. "Didn't you say that May can be a bad month?"

"It can, and we probably will get a storm or two, but the foals are all healthy and sturdy, as I think you just found out."

Wendy laughed. "They sure are strong enough," she agreed.

"The late spring snows usually don't last long, and the mares are tough. If things were too bad, we could feed, but the only real danger would be to a very young foal or an animal trapped in a canyon or gully, and I've fenced off those areas."

"Like the cliffs?" Wendy asked.

Uncle Art nodded. "I used to let the cattle roam through there, but one spring I lost a couple of head in one deep cut. I don't know how they happened to wander into it, but they couldn't get out when the blizzard hit. It was a week before I could get out there through the snow, and it was too late to save them."

Wendy shivered, thinking about Gypsy. If she hadn't gone after her, the filly might have tumbled into one of the gullies herself. Next time she wanted a hike, Wendy vowed, she'd take a piece of rope out and tie the gate shut. To banish further thoughts of Gypsy's being hurt, Wendy hurried in to play with Abigail's kittens before dinner.

"Have you decided yet which one we should keep?" Aunt Laura asked, watching the three balls of dark fluff as they rolled across the floor. Their eyes were just opening, but they were full of energy.

162

"What will happen to the other two?" Wendy asked.

"Peg Carter wants one, and I think the dairy is in the market for the other. Seems like some years nobody wants a kitten, and other years everybody does. Abigail picked a good year to produce a family."

Wendy studied the kittens. "I guess the black one should go to the dairy," she said. "He's the toughest already." She laughed as he attacked her finger. "Bootsie is going to be the prettiest, so I'm sure Mrs. Carter will like her. That leaves Little Bit for us."

"Little Bit?" Aunt Laura raised a questioning eyebrow.

Wendy picked up the smallest kitten. "She's got a little bit of every color on her," she explained. "See—brown, black, gold, cream, and even a white throat."

"Little Bit it is," Aunt Laura said with a grin. "Now how about giving me a hand with supper?"

The rest of the week passed in a busy haze. Wendy had little time for unhappy thoughts as she spent every day working with Uncle Art, Cliff, and George. Under their guidance, she

163

began learning firsthand the delicate art of training a horse.

She helped to introduce the young animals to the feel of a light bit in their mouths and to the first steps of reining; their feet and legs were handled constantly, to get them used to being brushed and combed.

Gypsy was included in the lessons, and Wendy was delighted to find that the filly learned faster than any of the other horses. Only two things kept Wendy from spending every waking minute in the corrals with Gypsy—the enforced two hours of study in the morning, and darkness at night.

It was Tuesday again when Aunt Laura interrupted Wendy's letter-writing to announce a change in their plans for the day. "Peg called," she said, "and she wants us to stop by her house about five tonight instead of going to the school."

"Maybe we could put it off till tomorrow," Wendy suggested hopefully.

"No, I think we'd better go today." There was something secretive about her aunt's smile. "Why don't you wear your new pantsuit?" she suggested a few minutes later, confirming Wendy's suspicion that something was up.

"What's so special about this trip?" Wendy asked, putting aside the letter she was writing to her father.

"I just thought you might like to show off your handiwork," Aunt Laura said.

Wendy sighed, sensing that there was more but not knowing how to go about finding out what it was. "All right," she said. "I've got to help with the yearlings before I get dressed."

"Better leave your letter then," her aunt said. "You'll have more to add later, anyway."

"I guess I'd better quit," Wendy agreed. "I'm going to have to mail this letter in a box instead of an envelope!" She picked up her sweater and headed quickly for the door, her thoughts already on Gypsy.

## 12 · Horse Killer

As SOON AS she saw the cars parked in front of the Carters' ranch house, Wendy knew that the meeting this evening wasn't going to be about her lessons. "Who's in there?" she asked.

Aunt Laura smiled. "Carol invited most of the young people from the Saddle Club over for pizza, and she wanted you to come, too. They're going to talk about the ride a week from next Saturday."

"Why didn't you tell me?" Wendy asked, not getting out of the car.

"Because I was afraid you'd find an excuse not to come," her aunt admitted, "and Carol really wanted you to be here."

"Do you think that's fair?" Wendy asked, trying hard to keep from showing how awful she felt. "You know that I can't go on the ride, so

166

why should I have to come here and listen to them making plans?"

"Wendy, I'm sorry. I really thought you might enjoy it if you didn't have too much time to think about it. You had fun at the Saddle Club meeting, didn't you?"

Wendy swallowed hard, thinking about what she'd overheard then about the missing horses. "It was all right," she admitted, "but I don't like getting involved in something I don't belong in."

"If you really don't want to go in—" her aunt began, but the door opened, and Kirk came out on the porch.

"Hi, Wendy. Come on in!" he called.

Wendy looked helplessly at Aunt Laura.

"I'm sorry," her aunt said. "I guess I made a mistake."

Wendy sighed. "It's just that no one understands how I feel," she said as she slid out of the car.

"We were about to call your house," Kirk said when Wendy reached the porch. "Everyone else is here."

"Sorry. What's going on, anyway?" Wendy forced herself to speak.

"We were just planning our ride, and we

wanted to make sure you were included. It's going to be a steak fry by the lake." Kirk opened the door, and Wendy was nearly driven back by a blast of music and voices and the strong smell of pizza that filled the room.

"Kirk, I really can't talk about the ride," Wendy began, knowing that she must end this now, before she got any more involved.

"Why not?" Carol came out into the hall, smiling.

Wendy swallowed hard, trying not to see the honest offers of friendship that were mirrored in Carol's and Kirk's faces. "Because I can't be a part of it," she said as firmly as she could.

"I don't see why not," Kirk said. "You can ride, can't you? And your uncle has plenty of horses."

"It's not that," Wendy began, conscious now of other faces as the rest of Carol's guests came out to greet her. For a moment it was like that day at school—the new faces seemed to blend into the well-remembered ones from Phoenix. They were staring, friendly now, but when they knew the truth. . . . Wendy began to feel sick from the food smells.

"Is it us, then?" Carol asked, her voice coming through the noise. "Don't you want us for your friends? Every time I see you, I ask you to ride over and visit, but you've never come or called or anything."

Wendy couldn't stand to look at the curious faces. She shook her head. "Please . . ." she said, "I don't feel well. May I call my aunt to come back for me?"

Carol said nothing, but Wendy could see the anger in her face as she pointed to the phone. In a moment the hall was cleared; the curious crowd was gone, and Wendy was alone with her guilt—still alone, as she had been since Buck's death. Knowing that her aunt wouldn't even be home yet, Wendy huddled in the chair by the phone.

She'd made a fool of herself, she realized. She hadn't explained. This was worse than her running away from everyone in Phoenix. At least, they knew why. . . .

Not that it mattered, Wendy told herself firmly. It would have happened anyway, no matter what she'd said. Everyone in this horse-crazy crowd would have been like Gretchen, once they found out about her killing Buck.

Blinking back tears, Wendy reached for the phone, but before she could dial, Kirk came back

169

into the hall. "Can I talk to you for a minute?" he asked.

Swallowing hard, Wendy nodded. "I'm sorry if I upset your party," she said.

"I'm sorry, too," he said. "It was as much my idea as Carol's. We thought you'd like to get to know everybody. I know we don't compare to your big city crowd, but—"

"Please," Wendy said. "I—it's not like that. It's not any of you. It's me. I don't belong here. This is all wrong for me. I just can't get involved in it."

For a moment she thought Kirk would give up and go back to the others, but he persisted. "I don't get it," he said. "Why can't you belong?"

"Because I can't ride." The words were said quickly.

"You can learn. Heck, half the gang can't ride real well, but they try."

"That's not what I mean. I know how; I just don't want to."

"But you like horses. I saw you with that filly and—"

"I can't ride. That's all there is to it." Wendy felt a flicker of panic at his persistence.

"We have dances and other stuff." Kirk's voice still held a note of questioning, urging her to

help him understand what was wrong.

"I'll be here only for a year, and then I'll be moving to wherever my father's job takes him," Wendy said, "so there's no use—"

"So we're not even good enough for a short-term friendship." Now there was anger in Kirk's voice. "Well, I'm sorry we bored you with our idea of fun. Don't worry; it won't happen again."

"You wouldn't want me, anyway," Wendy blurted, stung by his words. "I killed a horse! Because I was dumb and careless, I let him get killed! That's why I can't be a part of this."

She stopped, horrified at her own words. Kirk stared at her for several seconds as he absorbed what she'd said. Then his face went blank, and he turned away without another word.

Wendy didn't follow him with her gaze, nor did she pick up the phone. Instead, she fought down the choking sobs that told her she'd failed again.

Not waiting to call for a ride, Wendy fled from the Carter house and ran down along the beach, stumbling from the twinges of pain her bad leg gave her. It was part of the punishment she deserved, she told herself. She let the darkness swallow her up.

The house was deserted when she finally reached it. Not even wondering where her aunt and uncle were, Wendy slipped off her shoes, soaked from running along the edge of the lake, then crept to her room and collapsed on the bed.

It was over an hour before she heard voices. Her door was thrown open and the light blazed on cruelly, glaring into her tear-burned eyes.

"Wendy! Thank God you're here," her aunt said. "We've been driving around for hours looking for you. After Peg called, we were frantic."

"I'm sorry," Wendy said, adding this new guilt to her others.

"I'm glad you're okay," Uncle Art said gruffly, appearing behind Aunt Laura for a moment.

Aunt Laura closed the door and came over to sit on the bed. "Can you tell me what happened?" she asked.

"They wanted to be friends," Wendy answered tearfully, memory of it sweeping over her.

"Is that so terrible?" her aunt asked. "Wouldn't you like that?"

Wendy nodded. "More than anything. But it's too late now. They won't want to be friends anymore. I don't belong here."

"I thought you liked the ranch and living here

173

with us. I know you've been upset about not riding, but in time—"

"It doesn't matter about that anymore," Wendy said. "They know about me now—at least, Kirk does—and he'll tell all the others. Not riding is only part of it. It's killing Buck that they won't forgive."

"I don't understand. What has the accident to do with the young people here?" Her aunt looked honestly confused.

"It wasn't just an accident. Don't you see? Gretchen knew. It was my fault. Everyone told me to be careful, but I took Buck away from the riding areas. I was so busy pretending he was my own horse, I didn't even realize where we were. When he got scared, I just sat there and let it happen. I let him run into that truck. It was my fault—I have no business riding horses."

Her aunt said nothing for a long time, letting Wendy sob out the loneliness that seemed to be overflowing inside her.

"Do *you* hate me, too?" Wendy asked when she caught her breath again. "I'd understand, really. I understood when Gretchen never came to see me. I don't blame her any more than I blame Kirk and Carol for not wanting to be

174

around someone who'd do such a thing."

Aunt Laura stirred. "I love you, Wendy," she said softly. "We both love you very much. Did Kirk or Carol actually say—"

"No—" Wendy's voice broke— "but I know how they must feel."

"I can understand your guilt and sadness about what happened to Buck." Her aunt spoke slowly, choosing her words with care. "We always feel that way when something hurts the ones we love. We feel guilty because there's nothing we can do to prevent—"

"But it *was* my fault," Wendy reminded her.

"It's your fault that Gypsy's alive, too," her aunt said. "She'd have died a terrible death in that tangle of wire if you hadn't come along. She trusted you. No one else could have saved her."

"What if I do something to hurt her?" Wendy asked, fighting her longing to believe her aunt's words.

"What if you were riding Gypsy and she stumbled and you were badly hurt—would you blame her?"

"Well, no, but—"

"Wendy, when you love someone or something, that's part of the risk. When we asked you

175

to come here, we knew we'd grow to love you, and we knew how much it would hurt if you decided to leave us. But we thought it was worth it. We're glad you're here for us to love and care for."

"You still want me here?"

"If you want, you can stay forever."

"But Daddy—"

"Your father loves you very much, and you know that. But he thinks a girl needs more than just a father—especially when he travels so much."

Wendy nodded.

"Your father would let you stay here with us permanently if he were sure that you'd be happier with a secure home, instead of always moving around."

Wendy lay back, letting the strange warmth wash over her. It was love, she realized—love and understanding. She felt safe, till she remembered what had happened at the party. "You understand, but Kirk and the others never will."

"I made a mistake, and you're the one who's hurt by it," Aunt Laura said. "But I think you're judging Carol and Kirk unfairly."

Wendy shook her head. "I can't face them

176

again. My best friend couldn't forgive what I did to Buck. How could Carol or Kirk? If things were different. . . ."

Her aunt reached out and gently smoothed back Wendy's hair. "How about giving it some time?" she said. "Things have a funny way of working out—if you just let them."

Wendy smiled a little sadly. "I guess I'll have plenty of time," she said. "At least, I won't have any friends to keep me too busy."

"Don't give up hope. It's important for you to know that things will work out."

Wendy nodded, but she was a long way from sure that she could match her aunt's confidence in the future. After today, there seemed few rays of hope ahead.

A week passed, and after the strain of the first few days, Wendy fell back into the ranch routine, trying to lose herself in working with the horses. Gypsy was her joy and her defense against the loneliness that seemed to creep in when she least expected it. Without the filly, she knew she wouldn't be able to endure living here, no matter how wonderful her aunt and uncle's love was for her.

177

The time when she was to take her final exams was drawing near, and Wendy began spending several hours each night studying in her room. Her aunt and uncle usually had cheerful conversation for her when she was through studying, but on this Tuesday night, their faces were solemn. Uncle Art switched off the TV the minute Wendy stepped into the living room.

"What's the matter?" she asked. "Has something happened to Gypsy?" Tying gates had become a habit, but Wendy still feared that she might forget.

"Gypsy's safe in the barn, Wendy," Uncle Art assured her, "but it is about her. Sit down, honey, and listen."

Feeling suddenly cold, Wendy sank into one of the soft chairs. Aunt Laura set a cup of hot chocolate before her, but Wendy's hands were shaking, and she couldn't even pick it up. "What's happened?" she asked.

"Mr. Raither called this evening," Uncle Art began. "You remember—he's vice-president of the Saddle Club."

Wendy swallowed hard, remembering him all too clearly from the Saddle Club kitchen. She nodded, afraid of what was coming.

"It seems that his son mentioned Gypsy. He must have heard you talking about finding her in the wire."

Again Wendy nodded, feeling even colder.

"Anyway, he told me about a man in Idaho who raises Morgans. He's been advertising—offering a reward for the return of a couple of stolen horses. There was a telephone number with the ad; Mr. Raither gave it to me, and I telephoned the man."

Wendy looked down at her hot chocolate, unable to bear the pity that she saw in her aunt's face.

"I called him just a while ago," Uncle Art went on. "His name is Benson, and, sure enough, the filly is his. She was stolen, along with a mare. Mr. Benson was real happy to know we'd found the filly but disappointed that the mare wasn't with her. The mare is an older one that carries top bloodlines, and she was almost due to have a foal by a fancy Eastern stallion."

"I suppose he wants Gypsy back." It wasn't really a question.

"Of course he does," Uncle Art said. "He's flying up tomorrow to make arrangements and to see if he can't find out how or where she got

179

away from the thieves. He still hasn't given up the hope of finding the mare."

"Tomorrow?" It was almost a sob.

"We'll talk to him about Gypsy," Aunt Laura said. "Maybe he'll be willing to sell her. I really think it's mainly because of the mare that he's coming."

"Now, don't get your hopes up too high," Uncle Art warned. "She's a purebred Morgan, Wendy. They're worth a lot of money."

"I'd pay *anything*," Wendy said. "Daddy left a lot of expense money, didn't he? He'll send more if I need it. You will ask—offer to buy Gypsy—won't you, Uncle Art, please?"

"Of course I will, honey," he said. "I want Gypsy here, too. She's a silly filly, but she's got the makings of a fine horse for you, and that means a lot to us, you know."

Wendy looked at them, knowing that they sympathized and would do what they could. Slowly, totally swallowed by her own dark cloud of grief, she went to bed, wishing that tomorrow would never come.

## 13 · Blizzard!

MORNING CAME, in spite of her wishes. Wendy tried to go on through the day just as though her world weren't ending. She spent every spare moment of the morning with Gypsy, petting and grooming her, then giving her the usual work-out on the long rope.

The sky seemed to reflect Wendy's feelings, as did the damp, cold wind that sent probing fingers through her jacket, seeking to chill her skin. About noon, as Wendy was working one of the yearling Appaloosas, Aunt Laura called her to the phone. Hurriedly, Wendy put the colt and Gypsy (who served as an audience to the other young horses' training) in the corral.

"Wendy," Mrs. Carter said on the phone, "I've just been talking to the principal about your request to take the final exams a week before the rest of the class. He's agreed to it. Do you think you could be ready in two weeks?"

Wendy tried to force her mind to concentrate on something that now seemed so unimportant. "I guess so," she said. "I think I'm almost caught up on everything now."

"You seem to be," Mrs. Carter agreed, "and I'm very pleased with your work. I wouldn't recommend such a brief program for most of my students, but you had an excellent background to build on, so it didn't matter."

"I'm glad I'll be able to finish up before our first guests arrive," Wendy said automatically. "Aunt Laura will need me at the ranch then."

"Well, I'll tell the principal that we can go ahead with our plans to have you take the tests. See you Tuesday."

"What was that about?" Aunt Laura asked when Wendy hung up. "Did Peg decide you were caught up enough to take the tests early?"

Wendy nodded. "I'm going to take them in two weeks." She tried to sound pleased, but her heart was too heavy.

"Will you please call Art and the men in for lunch?" Aunt Laura asked. "We have to eat a little early. Cliff and George are going to drive

182

to Missoula to pick up a bull Art bought just before you came, and we have to drive into town to wait for Mr. Benson. He's flying his own plane, so we don't know exactly what time he'll get here . . . just that it will be in the afternoon.''

Wendy looked at her aunt sadly. "Would it be all right if I stayed here with Gypsy?" she asked.

"I'd rather you weren't alone this afternoon," Aunt Laura said. "I know how difficult the waiting is and how much Gypsy means to you—"

"That's why I can't leave her this afternoon," Wendy said, trying not to think that this might be her last afternoon with the filly.

"I understand. Still, I don't like the looks of the weather. I'd feel much better if there were someone here with you, but—"

"Is there a storm coming?" Wendy asked hopefully, thinking that it might delay Mr. Benson's arrival.

"I haven't heard anything about one yet," Aunt Laura said, "but I wouldn't be surprised. The weatherman doesn't always forecast the storms ahead of time. Art's always joking about shoveling two feet of 'partly cloudy' off the porch."

Wendy's smile nearly turned into tears, and

she fled from the kitchen to the front porch to call her uncle and the two ranch hands in for lunch. It seemed colder than it had been moments before, but Wendy decided it was because she'd been inside with her jacket on. Not that it mattered, anyway, she thought bitterly. When Mr. Benson took Gypsy away, nothing much would make any difference.

During lunch, nobody mentioned Gypsy, sensing Wendy's unhappiness. There were mumblings about the weather, and then the conversation turned to the trip into town for the newly purchased bull.

"Is it okay if I take my gelding along, boss?" George asked as he and Cliff finished eating. "The guy you bought the bull from was kind of interested in him."

"No problem," Uncle Art said. "The trailer's big enough for both of them."

"By the way, Art," Cliff said, "I turned my mare out with the herd. That bruise isn't healing as fast as I'd hoped."

"You can bring in one of the dude horses tomorrow," Uncle Art said. "Nobody's going to be riding today, anyway."

Uncle Art and Aunt Laura drove off in the

station wagon a few minutes after the men left. With mixed emotions, Wendy watched them go. The house seemed big and empty without the familiar sounds, and Wendy could understand why her aunt hadn't wanted her to be alone. But, she reminded herself bitterly, there was Gypsy . . . until after today.

Wendy pushed the thought away and hurried to finish clearing the table. She rinsed the dishes and put them in the dishwasher, then went to get a heavier sweater to wear under her jacket.

She started for the door, making a detour to the kitchen to turn off the radio. Just as she reached for the knob, the music was cut, and the announcer said, "I've just been handed a weather bulletin: a storm warning for you farmers and ranchers. Seems there's another spring blizzard blowing down out of Canada, and it's headed our way. It's advisable to get your calves and lambs and foals to some kind of shelter as quickly as possible. Now, back to our music. . . ."

Wendy looked at her watch. It was after one o'clock. Would the storm stop the plane somewhere else? She had no way of knowing. It would probably depend on when Mr. Benson had left Idaho, she decided, stepping outside.

185

The cold nearly took her breath away, but something else struck her, too: There were horses on the lawn! "Gypsy!" she cried, though the little filly was nowhere in sight. Wendy realized that, in her hurry to get to the phone before noon, she'd forgotten to tie the corral gate. It was standing open, and half the young horses were out.

As quickly as she could, Wendy started shooing the yearlings, the two-year-olds, and the one three-year-old back inside the corral. It seemed to take forever. Finally they were all in the corral —all but Gypsy. The filly had vanished.

Wendy whistled, and her heart lifted at the immediate sound of answering hoofbeats. She turned, and her hope drained away as a small pinto loped along the edge of the road and skidded to a stop in front of her. "Hi," Carol said from the saddle.

"What are you doing here?" Wendy asked, her disappointment turning to bitterness.

"Just riding through," Carol said, lifting her reins to turn the pinto.

Wendy swallowed hard. "I'm sorry, Carol," she said. "Please don't go."

For a moment the girl hesitated. Then she slid

186

off, dropping the reins to ground-tie her horse. "Mom told me last night," she said, "about your uncle finding Gypsy's owner." She stared at the ground, looking strangely shy. "I knew how you'd be feeling about losing her."

"My aunt and uncle didn't stop by and ask you to come over, did they?" Wendy asked, suddenly suspicious. "They just went to the airport to pick him up."

Carol shook her head. "No. I came on my own. Look, Wendy, if you'd rather be alone with Gypsy this afternoon, I'll understand. I just came over to tell you that I feel bad about it, too. We all do."

"Gypsy!" Wendy gasped, the shock of Carol's sudden arrival forgotten. "She's gone, Carol!"

"Gone? Where?"

Wendy closed her eyes, fighting a rising feeling of despair. "She's run away again," she murmured. "She opened the corral gate. I just got the other horses back inside."

"Where would she go?" Carol asked, glancing at the rapidly darkening sky.

Two agonizing thoughts struck Wendy— Gypsy on the lake cliffs, whinnying and pacing, then her uncle's words: *I lost a couple of head*

187

*in one deep cut. . . . It was a week before I could get out there through the snow, and it was too late. . . .*

"Do you know where she is?" Carol asked again, breaking into Wendy's thoughts.

Wendy nodded, her face as grim as her thoughts. "I think she's heading for the lake cliffs," she said.

"But your uncle has that fenced off, hasn't he?" Carol asked.

Wendy shook her head. "Gypsy opens gates. That's how she got out."

"We'd better get going, then," Carol said. "That storm isn't going to wait."

Wendy bit her lip. "I don't have a horse to ride," she said. "The dude horses and mares are in the lake pasture. George took his saddle horse, and Cliff's is lame."

"Happy's in, isn't he?" Carol asked.

"I couldn't ride him—" Wendy began. "Didn't Kirk tell you about me—about what I did to Buck?"

Carol nodded, her eyes sad but not accusing. She reached out to stroke her pinto's neck. "You could ride Quito, except that I've just started to train him. He's probably harder to handle than

188

Happy Warrior would be."

Wendy stared at Carol for several seconds, unable to find words for the feelings that stirred inside her. The thought that Carol would trust her with her own horse was like a guiding hand in the darkness.

"Are you going after her or not?" Carol asked at last, breaking the spell of silence.

"I'm going," Wendy said, heading for the barn at a trot. With her heart pounding like surf in her ears, she went to the tack room and got the stallion's bridle.

Happy Warrior seemed bigger than usual when he came trotting across the paddock. Wendy got him bridled and led him into the barn. Saddling him wasn't easy, even with Carol's help. When he was ready, Wendy was shaking so hard she could hardly lead him out of the barn.

*It was a week before I could get there . . . it was too late. . . .* Her uncle's words echoed ominously in her ears, driving her into action. Eyes shut, teeth set in her lower lip, Wendy put her foot in the stirrup and swung up onto the powerful stallion. She didn't wait for the sickness to come. A touch of her heels, and they were off

189

across the home pasture in a ground-eating lope, with Quito and Carol right behind them.

As expected, they found the gate open, telling Wendy that her suspicions about Gypsy's destination were correct. "She's headed for the cliffs, all right," Wendy said, not happy to be right.

"Why would she go there?" Carol asked as they were forced to slow the horses on a rough stretch.

"I think maybe she came in that way," Wendy explained. "And it could be that the missing mare is still out there. Uncle Art says there are lots of gullies and ravines that could trap a horse."

"You mean the mare that was stolen?"

Wendy nodded, then slowed Happy Warrior even more as they reached the rough stretch where Ladybug had fallen. The stallion had no difficulty going over the rocky ground, though. He paused to send a piercing whinny into the freezing wind, and there were answers immediately. Even before Wendy and Carol reached the second open gate, Gypsy appeared ahead, on the slopes of the lake cliffs.

This time Wendy didn't try to whistle the filly away. She'd heard the second whinny answering

Happy's call. There was another horse there, and, since it hadn't joined Gypsy, it must be trapped in the rough gullies or ravines below.

"Sounds like you guessed right," Carol said as they rode through the gate.

"I hope it is the mare," Wendy said. "Uncle Art said she's very valuable, and she may have a foal, too."

"Look!" Carol said as they reached the top of the bluff. She pointed beyond the spot where Gypsy was standing.

Wendy slid out of the saddle to pet Gypsy, then turned to look below. In a deep, L-shaped ravine stood a beautiful brown mare. Beside her stood a skinny, wobbly-legged foal, no more than a few days old.

"That's why you kept coming out here, Gypsy," Wendy said, patting the filly. "You wanted us to find your friends, didn't you?"

Gypsy whickered and moved away along the edge of the gully, looking back and obviously meaning for them to follow. Wendy remounted, and Happy Warrior moved forward.

"Do you think she knows where she's taking us?" Carol asked as they rode down along what appeared to be an old, unused road.

"I hope so," Wendy said, eyeing the lowering clouds. "I don't think we've got much time before the blizzard hits. We've got to get her out of there," she added, watching as the mare limped slowly along below them. "She doesn't look too good."

"There's not enough grass down there to feed her," Carol agreed. "She'd sure never survive another blizzard, and neither would that foal. He looks awfully young."

As the road curved down, Wendy caught sight of some sort of vehicle partially hidden in the brush. "What's that?" she asked, suddenly wondering if the thief might still be in the area.

"It looks like a horse trailer," Carol said, "or what's left of one. Look how the side's bashed in."

"Do you suppose that's how they got left here?" Wendy halted the stallion beside the trailer. "It doesn't look as if it could be hauled now."

Carol, who had ridden on ahead to the fallen tree where the filly stood, nodded her agreement. "It looks like the thief had an accident, wrecked his trailer, and put the horses in this ravine to keep them out of sight. He dragged this old tree down here to block the entrance to the ravine."

Wendy joined her, looking across the lightning-blasted pine into the ravine. The mare appeared from around a stony outcropping and came to the barricade with no sign of fear. "How did Gypsy get out?" Wendy wondered aloud.

Carol shrugged. "I'll bet that Gypsy jumped right over this log," she said. "The mare wouldn't be able to jump, carrying a foal, and now she's too weak. We've got to get them out before the storm hits."

Wendy nodded, shivering as the icy fingers of the wind penetrated her jacket. She tugged at one of the projecting limbs, but the tree didn't stir. "How?" she asked as a snowflake drifted down onto her cheek.

Carol sighed, chewing her lower lip. "There isn't time to go for help," she said. "And we can't drag her up the walls. She'd break a leg, for sure."

Wendy looked around, desperation beating in her like a pulse. If they didn't get the mare and foal out of the gully before the storm hit, the two were doomed. Her eyes lit on the heavy rope fastened at one side of Happy's saddle. "Maybe we can pull the tree out," she suggested.

Carol looked doubtful but hurried to free her own rope. Choosing the smaller end of the trunk, the girls knotted the two ropes in place, then tied the free ends to their saddle horns. Wendy mounted the stallion and turned him away, slowly riding out the slack.

The moment the rope tightened, Happy swung around to face the tree, backing just enough to keep the line taut. The tree didn't budge, not even with the much-lighter, untrained pinto pulling.

"That's not going to do it," Carol said. "The thief must have used a car to drag it."

"If Happy would only pull—" Wendy said.

"He's been trained to work cattle, not to haul," Carol said. "You can't expect him to drag it."

"He's got to try," Wendy said. The snowfall was heavier now, warning that time was growing short.

Wendy turned the stallion away from the log and touched him with her heels. Happy responded till he felt the heavy tug of the rope, then started to turn once more, they way he had been trained. "No!" Wendy said, reining him

194

away. "Pull, Happy! Pull hard!"

The stallion obeyed, bunching his heavy haunches and throwing his vast muscles hard against the rope. For a terrible moment, Wendy wondered which would give first—the saddle, the horse, or the rope. Then, with a rumble, the trunk shifted and slid away from the opening.

"We did it!" Wendy shouted, sliding off the stallion as Carol rode Quito up beside her. Together they freed their ropes and hurried around the end of the log.

The mare was gentle and easy to catch, and it took only a moment to fashion the rope into a halter for her. As they worked, Wendy could see healing wounds on the mare's shoulder, undoubtedly caused by the crash of the horse trailer. She realized that the welts on Gypsy's side had come from the same accident. She'd been frightened and hurt, and that could account for her fear of men, too.

As Carol led the mare around the tree trunk, the foal scrambled after his mother, his too-long legs going in all directions and nearly dropping him to the ground.

"You'd better lead the mare," Carol said. "Quito's so green he's liable to tangle the rope and panic." Knowing that Gypsy and the foal would follow, Wendy took the lead rope and mounted Happy. They started quickly for home.

Their elation over rescuing the horses was dimming by the time they reached the first gate. The lame mare could scarcely trot, and the foal already showed signs of weakening. The snow was coming faster now, nearly hiding the ground ahead. Gypsy kept appearing and disappearing in the shifting storm.

"We'd better stop a minute," Carol said. "We're going to lose the foal and each other in this snow."

"I don't think he's going to make it," Wendy said, her heart aching for the little creature as he stood, shivering, against his mother's side.

Carol looked around thoughtfully. "Could you hold him on the saddle in front of you?" she asked.

"On Happy?"

"He'd let you," Carol said. "He's well trained. I'd try Quito, but he's only been ridden for about three weeks now. He's pretty green."

"I'll try," Wendy said, "but how can we get him up here? Happy's a big horse."

"First let's get everybody tied together," Carol

suggested. "Once the wind really starts, we won't have a chance." She took her rope, ran it through the ring on Gypsy's halter, then tied one end to Quito's bridle and the other to Happy's saddle horn.

In the meantime, Wendy surveyed the area till she spotted an outcropping of rock just ahead. It looked about saddle height, and when she pointed it out, Carol nodded. "That'll have to do," she said.

Together they half dragged, half carried the foal up onto the rocks. Carol held him there while Wendy rode Happy into position. "What do you want me to do?" Wendy asked.

"Wrap your reins around the saddle horn so you don't drop them, then slide back out of the saddle. I'll shove the colt off, but you'll have to get him across. Think you can do it?"

Wendy bit her lip but nodded her agreement. It was a crazy, desperate scheme, and if it didn't work—if Happy got scared and decided to fight— Wendy pushed the thoughts away, knotting her reins as Carol had instructed, then sliding back behind the saddle. "Steady, Happy. Stand, boy," she said as Carol pushed and lifted the struggling foal over the edge of the rocks. Wendy

198

gasped as a flailing hoof caught her in the stomach. Then she got one arm around the foal's chest and the other around his thin haunches and struggled to ease him down in front of her.

Happy ducked a little, as if preparing to buck, then steadied as Wendy stroked his shoulder and murmured words of praise. The foal, apparently exhausted by his struggles, lay motionless across the saddle in front of her.

Carol, rubbing tenderly at her hip, ran to mount Quito. "Let's go!" she shouted as she swung into the saddle. "You take the lead, Wendy, and I'll try to keep the rope taut so we don't get tangled up."

Suddenly the wind came, howling like a fiend through the trees, driving the snow at them horizontally. The world disappeared behind a wall of white. Wendy, who'd been about to spur Happy into action, sat paralyzed. The trail to the ranch was gone. She couldn't see Carol or Gypsy. She was alone.

Happy began walking slowly, without Wendy's urging, and the two ropes tightened over her legs. The others were still behind her, though they'd vanished in the awful whiteness. Wendy leaned forward to make sure that the ends of the reins were still knotted on the saddle horn, then opened her jacket and tried to cover as much of the foal as she could.

"It's up to you, Happy," she shouted into the storm. "You'll have to take us home."

# 14 · One Blue Eye

NUMBNESS SET IN, shutting out all sensation beyond the cold. Time and motion slowed gradually into white stillness. Even the snowflakes seemed to hang suspended in the air, in a dazzling white fog.

Wendy realized that Happy wasn't moving. She straightened up, forcing her ice-caked eyelids open. Something dark was looming ahead of them. Happy moved a little, and Wendy recognized the gate. Stiffly, struggling to reach around the still motionless little foal, she leaned down to unlatch it.

Happy moved through, not turning back for her to close and latch the gate as he'd been trained to do. He just kept moving forward, head down, plodding against the icy wind that drove the ice-spiked snow like a thousand needles into his skin. Wendy closed her eyes again, wondering when she would finally become too cold to hold on. Would they find her later, frozen in a snowdrift, with the foal beside her? Were the ropes connecting her with the others still taut? Was Carol still back there, riding blindly as she was doing? And Gypsy—was the filly somewhere in this white nightmare world?

Wendy drifted into a dream, picturing herself galloping across a field of white flowers. She was riding Gypsy, and there was no one to stop her to take the filly away. They were flying together in the warm bright sun; Gypsy was hers, and she was unafraid, laughing to the rhythm of hoofbeats.

A sharp, ringing neigh brought Wendy back to freezing reality. Happy had stopped again. This time something huge loomed up in front of her. The barn? Wendy asked herself, trying hard to pry her half-frozen fingers loose from the saddle. She must get down and open the door; then they wouldn't freeze. But Wendy couldn't move.

Slowly, as in a dream, the door before her rose, and light spilled out.

"Good Lord!" Uncle Art said. "You were right,

Laura; you did hear a horse. Here, help me get her into the garage."

Wendy shook her head, realizing it was the garage door that Happy had brought her to, not the barn. Happy walked in, and another man, a stranger, started to close the door. "Wait," Wendy croaked, trying to pull the ropes that were frozen to her jeans. "Carol! Horses!"

In a moment three more white-crusted shadows drifted into the light. "My mare!" the strange man shouted. "And my filly!"

"Carol!" Aunt Laura gasped, running to where Quito had stopped.

"Not to mention a foal," Uncle Art said, lifting down first Wendy, then the foal.

Wendy leaned against the station wagon, too weak to stand. A dozen questions flew at her, but she could only breathe in the warm air and stare at Carol and the snow-covered horses. Finally Aunt Laura said, "For heaven's sake, leave them alone till they thaw out. Come on, girls, let's get some hot chocolate into you while I run a couple of warm baths. You must be nearly frozen."

"You'd better call Mom," Carol said weakly. "She'll be frantic."

"Gypsy?" Wendy forced the word out between chattering teeth.

"We'll take care of the horses, honey," Uncle Art said. "You can tell us the whole story later."

For a while it was like a dream again. Wendy was conscious of Carol's presence nearby and of her aunt's hands and voice. She followed each of Aunt Laura's commands automatically, not thinking beyond the moment. Drinking the steaming hot chocolate, taking off her ice-stiff clothing, lying in the lukewarm water as it was slowly heated—it was all part of the dream. Only when she was once more dressed, in warm wool slacks and two heavy sweaters, did Wendy begin to be fully aware of what was going on.

"How do you feel?" her aunt asked as the three of them stood in Wendy's room.

"My fingers and toes are still tingly, and my face hurts a little, but otherwise I'm okay. How about you, Carol?"

"I'm thawing out fine." Carol turned to Aunt Laura. "Did you call Mom?" she asked.

Aunt Laura nodded. "She thought you were at the Donahues, so she hadn't been worried. When I told her where you'd been, she was pretty shaken. I think you should call her before long."

Carol nodded. "I'm glad I didn't tell her I was coming over here," she said, looking shyly at Wendy. "I wasn't sure I'd make it when I started out," she admitted.

"I'm glad you did," Wendy said. "I couldn't have done it without you, Carol."

Carol's frost-reddened cheeks darkened a little, but her grin was warm. "That's what friends are for," she said.

Wendy grinned back. "What about the horses?" she asked her aunt.

"Why don't we go see?" Aunt Laura suggested, smiling widely. "Art and Mr. Benson must be anxious to know just what happened. So am I."

The attached garage, half-empty with the pickup truck gone, had been converted into a heated stable. Mr. Benson was rubbing down the mare, and just as they walked in, Uncle Art came through the big door, covered with snow and bent under the weight of a burlap bag. "Here are the oats," he said. "Some hay, too."

"How did you find your way to the barn?" Wendy asked, wide-eyed.

"I strung a rope between here and there before the blizzard hit," he said. "We beat it home by about half an hour. Long enough to discover you, Gypsy, and Happy missing—but not long enough to do anything about it. Even the sheriff couldn't help us search till after the storm. What happened?"

It seemed to take forever to tell the story and answer all the questions, but at last Carol and Wendy were free to turn their attention to the horses. Gypsy, Happy, and Quito seemed none the worse for their terrible journey. When Wendy saw the way Mr. Benson stroked Gypsy's sides, she knew that he'd never abused the filly. Still, her heart was heavy as she watched him. It seemed obvious which of the horses he loved best.

"Do you think your mare will be all right?" Wendy asked.

"I think so," Mr. Benson said. "She must have been hurt in the trailer accident, but her shoulder has healed pretty well. She's thin from being trapped without food. I can't understand how the thief could just go off and leave her there to starve."

"It's hard telling what happened to him,"

Uncle Art said. "He might have been injured in the accident, too. It's just lucky that Gypsy got out. I seldom ride that way, so I sure wouldn't have found the mare in time to save her."

"What about the foal?" Carol asked. "He's so weak and tiny."

Uncle Art smiled. "Newborn foals usually are," he said. "That little fellow isn't more than a day or so old, which is probably just as well. If he'd been any bigger or stronger, I doubt that the two of you could have gotten him onto Happy or held him there."

"Do you think he'll be all right?" Wendy asked, remembering how still he'd been on the journey through the blizzard.

"I'll want them both examined by a veterinarian as soon as the blizzard is over," Mr. Benson said, "but I'm pretty sure they'll recover—thanks to you girls."

"I can't take any credit," Carol said. "I just went along for the ride. Wendy's the one who figured out where Gypsy'd gone—and why."

"It was Gypsy that led us to them," Wendy said. "She'd gone there before, but I was too dumb to investigate. The credit should go to her—and to Happy." She went over to scratch

207

the neck of the big stallion. "If it hadn't been for him, we couldn't have gotten them out of the gully at all, and even if we had, I'd never have been able to find my way home."

"He's a remarkable horse," Mr. Benson said. "It's unusual for a girl your age to be riding a stallion."

Wendy giggled a little at the words. "I did ride him, didn't I?" she said. "It seems so long ago. I was worried at first, but after we found the mare, I didn't have time to think. The snow was already starting, and we just had to get them home."

"Well, you did," Mr. Benson said. "I offered a thousand-dollar reward to anyone who could help me recover my horses, and, of course, that will go to you two girls. I really can't tell you how grateful I am."

Wendy looked at Mr. Benson, suddenly realizing that he was the man she'd hated and feared for so long—Gypsy's rightful owner! "Mr. Benson," she said, "is Gypsy for sale?"

"The filly? I don't think so. I explained to your aunt and uncle that her breeding is the finest."

"But I love her, and she loves me," Wendy said. Her voice rose as her desperation increased.

"I found her trapped in the barbed wire . . . and then she nearly died from the infection . . . and, well, we're just meant to be together. I've even been training her, and—" Wendy's words were lost in incoherence as she realized that she was losing the filly.

Gypsy, her oats gone, came over to lean her dainty head against Wendy's chest. She didn't mind the tears that dripped from Wendy's chin onto her blaze face.

Mr. Benson shook his head. "That filly would be worth several thousand dollars," he said. "If it weren't for her mismatched eyes, that is. That blued eye could be passed on to her foals. I suppose—" he paused, studying Gypsy thoughtfully—"I could let you have her for . . . uh, five hundred dollars."

Wendy was smiling and crying and hugging the filly all at once. She could only nod her head in agreement.

"Well, young lady," Mr. Benson said, turning to Carol, "I guess I owe you five hundred dollars, don't I?"

The garage filled with happy laughter.

"Well," Aunt Laura said, her usual matter-of-fact voice quavering a little, "I guess, now that

209

that's settled, we'd better see about something to eat. Would you give me a hand, Carol?"

Wendy felt as though the sun were shining inside her as she looked at the smiling faces around her. "I'll be right in, too," she said. "Just let me talk to my horse for a few minutes."

"No rush," Carol said softly.

# YOU WILL ENJOY

## THE TRIXIE BELDEN SERIES
28 Exciting Titles

## THE MEG MYSTERIES
6 Baffling Adventures

## ALSO AVAILABLE

Algonquin
Alice in Wonderland
A Batch of the Best
More of the Best
Still More of the Best
Black Beauty
The Call of the Wild
Dr. Jekyll and Mr. Hyde
Frankenstein
Golden Prize
Gypsy from Nowhere
Gypsy and Nimblefoot
Lassie—Lost in the Snow
Lassie—The Mystery of Bristlecone Pine
Lassie—The Secret of the Smelters' Cave
Lassie—Trouble at Panter's Lake
Match Point
Seven Great Detective Stories
Sherlock Holmes
Shudders
Tales of Time and Space
Tee-Bo and the Persnickety Prowler
Tee-Bo in the Great Hort Hunt
That's Our Cleo
The War of the Worlds
The Wonderful Wizard of Oz